The Silent Stalker

Charlotte Longoria

Copyright © 2024 by Charlotte Longoria

All rights reserved.

No portion of this book may be reproduced in any form without written permission from the publisher or author, except as permitted by U.S. copyright law.

Contents

1. Chapter 1 — 1
2. Chapter 2 — 8
3. Chapter 3 — 16
4. Chapter 4 — 24
5. Chapter 5 — 32
6. Chapter 6 — 40
7. Chapter 7 — 47
8. Chapter 8 — 54
9. Chapter 9 — 61
10. Chapter 10 — 68
11. Chapter 11 — 75
12. Chapter 12 — 82
13. Chapter 13 — 88

14.	Chapter 14	95
15.	Chapter 15	98
16.	Chapter 16	101
17.	Chapter 17	104
18.	Chapter 18	109
19.	Chapter 19	113
20.	Epilogue	117

Chapter 1

"You probably wonder what my story is about.." Let me introduce me a bit first, my name is Maddison, actually Maddison Delores to be precise. All my life I have lived in Las Vegas with my mother, people expect the best from me and that is what they get, but don't play games with me because you will regret it. They always say "Never walk alone in the dark."

Well... I didn't listened to that, if I had listened to that, I don't think I would be here at all, and then I don't think I would have found the love of my life. I'll tell you where it all started, it was about 5 years ago...

2017 september 5

-5 years ago-

It was midnight, 4am. Maddison wakes up because she has a bad dream she decides to go back to sleep, a little later she wakes up again, she can't fall asleep anymore and is wide awake, she looks at her phone and sees that it is 4 o'clock in the morning,

she looks outside and she sees that the wind is blowing hard, she gets out of bed and walks downstairs to get some water, she takes the glass and drinks a little bit of it, she puts the glass down again and decides to take a walk outside because she can't fall asleep, she puts on her coat and shoes and Maddison opens the door,

it's quite cold but Maddison still goes outside to walk at 4am. Maddison looks around and hears all kinds of strange noises, she regrets going for a walk but she still goes, she hears something in the trees, but luckily it was nothing.

A moment later, Maddison hears someone walking behind her, she looks back and sees no one. She wants to turn her head again and she sees someone standing from a distance, she starts to shake with fear. She wants to take her phone out of her pocket and the person starts walking towards her, she sees from the walk that it is a boy.

Maddison tries to call her mother but doesn't pick up, "help!" Maddison says, but the boy doesn't respond but just starts walking faster and faster towards her, she blinks her eyes and the boy is standing in front of her, Maddison is breathing heavily from fear. "What are you doing here all alone in the dark at night? You shouldn't be here." The boy says in a deep voice.

Maddison looks at him with fear in her eyes, she sees his eyes turn red, she looks with fear. "Your eyes, they're red.." She says in a dull voice. "Isn't that the point? " The boy says, showing his vampire teeth. "No, this can't be real, I think I'm dreaming! " thinks Maddison.

The boy wants to sink his vampire teeth into her neck, but just in time she escapes and runs as fast as she can, the boy uses his speed powers to catch up with her.

Maddison sees a large rock on the ground and picks it up, she throws the rock straight into his face and runs as fast as she can, the boy bleeds but the blood is also gone immediately. He can no longer see her and tries to look for her, but he can't see her anywhere. In the meantime Maddison is running for her life,

she can see the sun rising and she can see her house in the distance, just a few more steps and she is at her house, she looks back again or that she still sees the boy but luckily she doesn't see anything, a little later she is finally standing at her door completely exhausted, she is breathing heavily because she is so tired from running,

she quickly takes the keys from her pockets and opens the door, she takes of her shoes and jacket and closes the door. Maddison runs upstairs to her mother's bedroom, she opens the door, "Mom wake up!" Maddison says, her mother opens her eyes and says in a soft voice "honey what's wrong, why are you waking me up at 5 am?"

Maddison looks at her mother and says "I was attacked by a vampire...or maybe it was a werewolf!" Maddison's mom looks at her and starts laughing. "A vampire, or werewolf? Honey, I know 100 percent that that's not true and that it was just a dream, now go back to sleep, I have to get out of bed at 6 in the morning for work." Maddison's mom said. "Mom you're not listening! It wasn't a dream!" Maddison says angrily. Maddison's mom looks at her and says "Maddison go back to bed!"

Maddison sighs angrily and goes back to her room, she really can't get back to sleep after what happened. Maddison was completely confused and didn't know what to do, if Maddison told her friends they wouldn't believe her, she knew that straight away. She was still thinking about what it was, a vampire, werewolf, or maybe something else? She just wasn't sure.

Maddison was trying to remember what he looked like, but she really couldn't remember. Maddison got out of bed to get ready, even though it was half past six in the morning, she sat down on her desk chair and grabbed her makeup from her drawer and her brush to comb her hair. A little while later Maddison was ready for school, she got up and made her bed, she opened the curtains and opened the window for some fresh air.

Maddison walked downstairs but her mother was still sleeping, Maddison wasn't hungry for breakfast either, she was still shocked about what had happened last night, she didn't dare walk on the street or go to school anymore, but she went anyway , even tho she was so scared of the boy who attacked her last night, she thought he would attack her again.

Maddison had decided she would only tell her best friend about what happened last night, but she already knew she would never believe her.

Maddison was standing at the door to leave for school, she had already packed her bag and she opened the front door to go, she stepped outside and looked around to see if she saw anything,

luckily she saw nothing. Maddison closed the front door again and left for school. Moments later, she was still on her way to school and terrified that someone would attack her again. Maddison's best friend was calling her on the phone, Maddison took her phone out of her bag and answered it. "Where are you!?"

Says Maddison's best friend (Amelia) Maddison was confused and said "What do you mean, where are you? I'm really on time." Amelia said with an angry voice "It's 10 o'clock in the morning and school has already started!"

Maddison looked at the time and saw that it was already 10am, "no...that's not possible I was up at 5am! how can time go so fast?!" Maddison said, bewilderingly. "You better hurry because the teachers are gonna be pissed." Amelia said. "I'll be there in 5 minutes!" Maddison said and hung up. Maddison was running faster and faster to get to school, but she was still late.

A little later she was finally at school and she walked through the hallways, she looked around to see if she saw anyone, but everyone was already in class, Maddison opened the classroom door and everyone looked at Maddison. "Maddison Delores, you're late." The English teacher says, Maddison looks at the teacher and says "I know I'm late but I have a reason!" Everyone is looking straight into Maddison's eyes and waiting for a reason. "So.. I was up at 4am last night and something bad happened."

Maddison said in a low voice. "You peed in your pants or what?" A random boy says in her class. Everyone starts laughing but Maddison feels no shame because Maddison knows what really happened, but of course she isn't going to tell. "Yes, yes Maddison, I believe it again, now sit down quickly." Says the English teacher. Maddison walks to her spot in class past Amelia."You're lucky that the teacher didn't have a tantrum." Amelia says sarcastically.

Maddison sighs deeply and looks at Amelia. "I need to tell you something about what happened last night." Says Maddison. "What is it Maddy? you kissed a boy..?" Amelia says curiously. Maddison looks at her with wide open eyes and says."What, no!" Maddison takes a deep breath and says. "I was attacked by someone, I can't remember who or what it was but it was a boy, he had these very sharp canines and he wanted to bite me in the neck with those teeth! The whole class looks at Maddison and starts laughing. "Maddison Delores, to the director! I'm tired of these fairytale stories!"

Maddison sighs and gets up and grabs her things, Maddison walks to the door and she holds the door handle and wants to open the door, Maddison opens the door and she sees the most handsome boy she has ever seen standing in front of her. He had those ocean blue eyes and black hair, his face was just so perfect, Maddison kept staring at him because he was just too handsome.

"Can I pass? I have to be here in this classroom." Said the handsome boy. Maddison knew his voice from somewhere but didn't know from where. The boy walks past her and Maddison also recognizes his scent from somewhere, she couldn't remember where.

"Class I want everyone's attention, we have a new boy in our class, Jay Mendez."

Chapter 2

2017 september 5

"Class I want everyone's attention, we have a new boy in our class, Jay Mendez."

Of course all the girls were looking at Jay because he was just too handsome, Maddison walked over and closed the door, she walked through the hallways and looked around, it was super quiet because everyone had classes of course. Maddison didn't want to go to the headmistress at all, but she had to.

Maddison sees the headmistress room and walks towards it, she grabs the door handle and opens the door, as Maddison opens the door she sees a girl sitting with the headmistress, the thing is that the girl who was sitting looked exactly like Jay.

"Celina Mendez, I know you're only new to school today, but your behavior is already just like a 5 year old child, I want you to come for detention after 7th period. " Said the headmistress.

Maddison was just standing there and looking at them.

"But I don't want to go to detention, that's bullshit, just like you." Celina said. Maddison didn't expect that answer just like the headmistress. "That's enough Celina, i'm going to suspend you!" The headmistress said angry. Celina was angry and looked the headmistress straight in the eye.

"Now you're going to do as I say, you're going to give me my class schedule for today and stop bothering me, understand? Oh and by the way, I don't have to go to detention or get suspended." Celina said to the headmistress, it was like Celina was compelling her.

"I will do what you say, here is your class schedule for the day, good luck Celina! " Said the headmistress. It was like the headmistress was possessed. Maddison looked strange at them.

Celina looked at Maddison and gave Maddison this dirty look, Celina takes the class schedule from the headmistress's hands and stands up. Celina wants to walk to the door where Maddison is standing. Maddison and Celina looked at each other, "Aren't you Jay's sister?" Maddison asks. "Who knows." Celina says and she steps out the door and slams it shut.

Maddison walks to the table where the headmistress is also sitting, Maddison sits on the chair and looks at the headmistress, "How did she do that?" Maddison asked the headmistress. "What do you mean Maddison?" The headmistress said back. "You know what I'm talking about, the way Celina just said do this, do that, and you did it!" Said Maddison.

"Maddison, I have no idea what you're talking about, Celina never said that to me." Said the headmistress clearly.

Maddison looked confused and thought she was going crazy. "You know what, forget it, maybe it's just me." Maddison said disappointed. The headmistress looked at Maddison confused and said, "Anyway why are you here Maddison?" Maddison didn't want to tell what happened last night, Maddison was doubting herself whether it all really happened last night. "I don't know either, I think I talked too loudly in class, and I was also late." Maddison said.

"And why were you late?" The headmistress asked Maddison. Maddison didn't want to say it but she didn't know what else to say.

"I- I think i.. I WAS ATTACKED BY A CREATURE!" Maddison didn't wanna say that but it just came out of her mouth, Maddison regret what she said, the headmistress looked at Maddison like she was going crazy. "Eh .. April fools!" Maddison said awkwardly. "Maddison maybe you should just stay a day off, I don't think it's going well." The headmistress said to Maddison. Maddison had no idea what do say that she just stood up and took her bags and slammed the door right in front of the headmistress.

Maddison was walking through the school hallways. When the school bell rang, everyone came out of the classroom for recess. So Maddison knew that Amelia only had lesson until 5th period, so Maddison decided to wait for Amelia. In the meantime Maddison saw Jay walking trough the school hallways, Jay kept looking at Maddison. Maddison couldn't remember but she knew him from somewhere.

A little later it was 5th period, Amelia saw Maddison waiting for her and went to Maddison. "So, wanna get an ice cream?" Maddison said randomly. Amelia looked at her and said "Yeah sure..?" Maddison looked at Amelia and said "Look, I'll tell you what exactly happened but I can't tell it here." Maddison and Amelia got into Amelia's car to go get ice cream, "And I'm still so happy that you already have your driver's license." Maddison said laughing. "Why don't you have your license?" Amelia said. "Im still 17, duh." Maddison said back. And they drove to the ice cream shop.

In the meantime, The headmistress was thinking about what Maddison said earlier. The headmistress decides to call Madisons mom to tell her about what she said. The headmistress took the phone who was laying on her desk, and put Maddison's mom phone number in it.

"Hello who is this?" Maddison's mom said confused. "Good afternoon Celeste Delores, i'm the headmistress from your daughters school, i'm sorry that i'm calling so random! i wanted to talk to you about what happend, Maddison said something earlier and it was really strange.." The headmistress said to Celeste (Maddison's mom) "What did she say? " Celeste said to the headmistress on the phone.

"Well.. she said that she was attacked.. by a creature, i send her home because she was looking so pale at the same time as well!" The head mistress said to Celeste on the phone. Celeste started to believe about what Maddison said to her in the morning, Maddison said that she was attacked by a vampire or werewolf to Celeste.

"You know what, i will talk to Maddison about it! i'm sure she will feel better soon." Celeste said to the head mistress. "Okay then! have a good day, bye!" Said the head mistress, and the Headmistress hang up the phone.

In the meantime Maddison and Amelia were sitting on a bench eating an ice cream, "Okay so, last night I decided to go for a walk, and a boy attacked me! He had those vampire teeth and to be honest, it was a handsome boy, like really handsome, but he wanted to kill me!" Maddison said to Amelia. "Alright Maddy, im not gonna say that I don't believe you but.. the part that a boy attacked you I do believe, the vampire part I do not believe Maddy." Amelia said to Maddison. "But Amelia his eyes turned red!" Maddison said, "Maybe you just dreamed that they were red?" Amelia said. "You know what Amelia, I know that it seems not real, but I know what I saw!"

"Do you even remember what he even looked like?" Amelia asked Maddison. "Well I don't really remember but.. he had black hair, and that's pretty much what I remembered." Maddison said. Amelia and Maddison heard a car and saw two people coming out of it, Jay Mendez and Celina Mendez. "Isn't that the new boy and new girl at school?" Amelia said to Maddison. "Yeah, they are." Maddison said back while she was staring at Jay. "Maddy, I think that he is looking at you." Amelia said while she was looking at Jay. Maddison looked back at Amelia, "He is looking?!" Maddison said. "He keeps staring at you, not even us, just you!" Amelia said to Maddison.

Maddison was trying to not look at him, but he kept staring. Jay started to walk towards them. "Maddy, he. is. COMING!" Amelia said. Maddison was breathing heavily. "Well hello ladies, what a coincidence that you two are here, you both are in my class, right? " Jay said handsome. "Uh-m yeah we are." Maddison said stuttering. "Well my sister is getting me and herself an ice cream,

you two can sit with us if you'd like? " Jay said to Amelia and Maddison "Yeah we would like that! " Amelia said and she winked at Maddison at the same time, Maddison had her doubts about it but she does what Amelia says and goes to sit with Jay and Celina. "So where are you from?" Celina asked to Amelia and looked at Maddison dirty. "I was born in Los Angeles and we moved here when I was 4 years old." Amelia said to Celina.

"And what about you Maddison, where do you come from?" Jay asked Maddison. "I lived here all my life with my mom." Maddison replies back. "And your dad?" Celina said to Maddison and gives her this death stare. "I never met him." Maddison said, and there was a dead silence. "Maddison quick question, you were attacked last night I heard, do you know by who?" Jay asked.

Maddison looked at him confused, how could he know? And why this question? so many questions were going trough her head. "I know you from somewhere." Maddison said. "Oh, is that so? " Jay said questioning. Maddison's started to think deeply, she recognized him from somewhere, his voice, his walk, he had black hair as well.

It was him, it had to be, he attacked me! Maddison thought. Maddison looked at Jay and said, "Im sorry I have to go, my mom is going to pick me up right now, it was nice to meet you tho! Come on Amelia we're going." Celina looked at them strange. "Going this fast? " Celina asked. "Yeah her mom is gonna be pissed if she doesn't come home, right Maddy? " Amelia said, "Right." Maddison said back. Amelia and Maddison walked to somewhere random. "It was him." Maddison said. "What?! That's not possible, only cause he has black hair?" Amelia said back.

"No you don't understand Amelia, his voice, his walk, it's obvious!" Maddison said back. Amelia didn't reply on that. "Is your mom almost there to pick us up? " Amelia asked. "Yeah there she is." Maddison said, and they both walked to the car.

Maddison opened the door car and they both got in, "And girls? How was it? " Celeste asked. "Mom can you just drive to Amelia's house and drop her off? Right Amelia? " Maddison said, and Amelia nodded yes. "Alright then." Celeste said and she drove to Amelia's house. A little later they arrived at Amelia's house. "Thanks miss Delores for the drive, see you at school Maddy." Amelia said and she got out the car.

Maddison sighed, "Alright young lady, what is going on? I heard you were attacked, and yes I know you said that in the morning but at that point I didn't believed you but now I do, really." Celeste said. "Mom can we have this conversation tomorrow? Im pretty tired." Maddison said. "Tomorrow we will talk about it, I get that you're tired, when we're home you can rest." Celeste said to Maddison and she drove home.

They arrived home, and Maddison got quick out the car and opened the door with the keys, she took off her shoes and coat and walked upstairs, Celeste came in the house and closed the door. Maddison walked to the bathroom to wash her face, she looked in the mirror, "Am I seeing this? " Maddison said. She blinked with her eyes and looked again. "My eyes.. They're red!"

Chapter 3

2017 september 5

"My eyes.. They're red!" Maddison was freaking out. "Mom!" Maddison yelled at her mom. "My eyes!!" Maddison yelled again. Celeste ran upstairs and she opened the bathroom door, "What's going on?!" Celeste said to Maddison. "My eyes! Can't you see, they're red! " Maddison said in panic. "Red? They're not red Maddison." Celeste said back. Maddison looked in the bathroom mirror. "They were red I swear !" Maddison said to Celeste.

"Look honey, I get that your tired and seeing things that are not tru-" Said Celeste but she could not finish her sentence. "Mom i'm tired of people saying that i'm seeing things! I am not crazy, why would I even make this up? Mom if you're hiding something from me, then say it now or then I'll find out for myself." Maddison said mad.

Celeste did not knew what to say or do at this moment so she just left the room. Maddison was so disappointed in her mom, nobody listened to her. She started thinking, maybe that creep did it to me, Jay! Maybe that's the reason of those red eyes! Maddison decided to get in bed to get some sleep cause is has been such a long day, she played in bed and her eyes were slowly closing, a little later she fell asleep.

2017 september 6

The next day.. Maddison woke up from her alarm clock, she looked at the time and got out bed, she walked to the bathroom to look in the mirror, and no red eyes, just normal. She brushed her teeth and washed her face, she put some makeup on and was ready for school. Maddison tried to forgot what happened yesterday to get trough the day.

Maddison put on her shoes, she looked outside and the weather was pretty nice, so she didn't put a jacket on. She opened the door and looked outside, she stepped out the door and closed it. Maddison walked to school, she looked back if she saw anyone. Maddison looked right and she saw Jay walking. Maddison had no fear and decided to talk to him.

"Hey you, Jay! " Maddison shouted. Jay looked at Maddison and walked towards her. "Well hello Maddy." Jay said to Maddison, He called her Maddy, only Amelia called her that. "Don't act innocent Jay, I know what you did." Maddison said to Jay while they were both walking to school. "You aren't so scared of me are you? " Jay said. "Why would I? " Maddison said confused. "Well you know that I attacked you, right? Or was that a surprise? " Jay said to Maddison. Maddison looked at him, she was so angry at him, but she did not feel a fear.

"You will pay for what you did, because of you my eyes were red!" Maddison said. Jay looked confused at Maddison and started laughing. "Eyes, red? That's the lamest sh*t I've heard these years." Jay said. "Your eyes were red as well." Maddison said to Jay. "Look, you already know that I'm a vampire now and that I attacked you, I'm not gonna kill you cause that is boring, sooo.. I'm going to compel you to forget everything what happened that night! " Jay said and he took Maddison by the shoulders.

"September 5, you will now forget the night I attacked you, you will forget that I am a vampire, you will now forget everything about that night." Jay said while he was compelling Maddison. Maddison looked at him confused, "You freak!" Maddison said, and she escaped from him and ran. "Why didn't it work? " Jay asked himself.

Maddison was running, she had finally arrived at school, and this time not too late, Maddison saw Amelia standing by the lockers, Amelia looked at Maddison strangely "He tried to make me forget, I told you he's a vampire!" Maddison said exhausted. "Maddy can you stop acting like a 5 year old? Go write a book about vampires, then people might believe you. But I will not believe that crap." Amelia said and walked away.

Maddison felt like being stabbed in the back, how can she just walk away? Amelia was always Maddison's best friend since primary school, but they always say, you have to be okay with leaving people behind, some friendships aren't meant to last, Maddison did not feel like talking to Amelia today or the day after that, but she still had to sit next to her in class.

The bell rang, everyone walked to their class they had that moment, Maddison opened the door of her class where she had to be, she already saw Amelia sitting there, Amelia was talking with Celina Mendez, Jays sister. Maddison was trying not to look conspicuously at Celina and Amelia, Maddison took her spot next to Amelia, why would Amelia even talk to Celina?

So many questions were going trough Maddison's head. Celina and Amelia looked at Maddison. "Why are you sitting next to her." Celina asked to Maddison. "Because I can? And this is my seat, if Amelia doesn't want to sit next to me than she should go sit somewhere else." Maddison said back to Celina.

"You know what, I'm getting really tired of you, first you're making a story up that you got attacked by a vampire and now this?!" Amelia said mad to Maddison. The entire class was looking at Maddison. "Oh so now you're trying to embarrass me in front of the whole class?" Maddison said to Amelia.

Celina looked at Maddison and said "Look, not to ruin the scene but what do you mean a vampire attacked you?" Maddison looked at Celina, "Why would I tell you?" Maddison asked to Celina. "Because I'm curious and I want to know." Celina said mad.

"Class, everyone to your seats! We have a test today!" The English teacher said. Celina walked to her seat and Maddison and Amelia were sitting together. Maddison completely forgot about the test, if she fails this test she would get in trouble. The teacher was giving everyone their own test, "Now everyone quiet! And make the test! " The teacher said. Everyone was quiet and making the test. Amelia looked at Maddison.

Amelia was writing something on paper, not for the test. Amelia tapped Madison on her shoulder and she pointed to the piece of paper, there was a sentence on it. "Won't argue anymore?" that's what it said on the piece of paper, Maddison looked at the piece of paper that was next to Amelia's test. "Ma'am, she is cheating on my test!" Amelia said to the teacher. "What no! I wasn't I swear!" Said Maddison.

"Miss Delores I am sick of you, out of my class! You can catch up on the test after school." Said the teacher mad to Maddison. Celina and Amelia looked both at Maddison and laughed at her. Maddison was so mad but still took her stuff and left the classroom and slammed the door. Maddison was walking trough the hallways and walked to the bathroom,

She opened of the bathroom and Maddison looked in the mirror, "Listen to your emotions Maddison, they come with many lessons." Maddison said to herself, she tried to calm down because Maddison was so mad, she still got trough the day.

A little later it was 3pm, Maddison had to make the test cause she got send out the classroom second period because of Amelia, she walked to the classroom where she had to make the test, no one was there, she saw the test laying on the teachers desk with the answers,

this was Maddison's change, she closed the door and sat on the desk with the answers of her test, she was writing fast the answers on paper before anyone catches her, and a little later she was done with writing the answers on paper.

Maddison left the classroom and headed to the bathroom to fix her hair, she wanted to open the bathroom door and she saw Celina standing they're with Amelia. Celina grabbed Amelia by the throat, "What are you doing here Maddy?" Celina asked Maddison.

"Let Amelia go." Maddison said. "Why would I?" Celina said and Celina's eyes were turning red. Maddison was shocked. No not again.. Maddison thought, and she tried to escape, Maddison ran to the door and tried to open it, she grabbed the door handle and she saw Jay standing right in front of her and Jay had also red eyes. "Trying to escape?" Jay said to Maddison.

"W-what are you gonna do to me!?" Maddison said while stuttering. "We want to know something from you.'" Celina said to Maddison. "Like what?!" Maddison said confused. "Well you know, I tried to compel you, and it did not work, that means you're not a human." Jay said to Maddison. "What do you mean with that?" Maddison said.

"Us vampires can only compel humans, Jay tried compelling you and it did not work, so that means that you can't be a human, or you drink vervain tea." Celina said to Maddison. "I don't even know what vervain is?" Maddison said back.

"its this kind of herbs that vampires can't stand, they could die from it and it cancels compulsion." Celina said back to Maddison. "So, tell us why we can't compel you, or Amelia has to die right now." Jay said to Maddison.

Maddison looked at Amelia being scared. "No you can't do that!!" Maddison said mad. "Then tell us what you are!" Celina to Maddison. "I am human!" Maddison said back, and before she knew, they murdered Amelia right in front of Maddison.

Maddison couldn't believe her eyes. She was traumatized. "NO!" Maddison screamed. "Too late, you should've told us!" Celina said in a annoying way.

Maddison said nothing, she was still shocked. "So, we can't compel you to forget everything that happened, so we will clean up her body and if you tell someone a word about what happened, there will be a bad ending for you." Jay said and Celina and Jay left the bathroom with Amelia's body.

Maddison couldn't believe it, she refused to. Her best friend just died, well ex-bestfriend. Even tho they had an argument, she still did not wanted her to get hurt, Maddison really cared for Amelia and always will. Maddison left the bathroom and she knew that her mom would pick her up from school, Maddison tried to hold back her tears because she obviously didn't want anyone to see her cry.

Maddison saw her moms car standing over there, she walked to the car and opened the door car. Celeste looked at Maddison and said. "Ive been keeping a secret from you and it is time to tell you the truth."

Chapter 4

2017 september 6

"Ive been keeping a secret from you and it is time to tell you the truth." Maddison couldn't be more confused as what she was right now. "What do you mean a secret?" Maddison said to her mother (Celeste) "It all started when you were a baby.. When you were born Maddison, You had red eyes, the doctors couldn't believe it, but of course I already knew why it was." Celeste said. "Well go on .. say it." Maddison said. "I am a witch Maddison. Ive been keeping it a secret for too long and it was time to tell you the truth, now let me tell the story of the 4 kinds of witches." Celeste said. Maddison couldn't believe what she just heard.

"We have 4 kinds of witches, the Forest witches, fire witches, dobbelganger witches, and then you have the most powerful and the most dangerous kinds of witches, the blood witches. They are even that powerful, that they can kill themselves with over power. The blood witches don't exist anymore, until you were born. You are a blood witch Maddison." Celeste said.

Maddison had no words to say, she was speechless. "And why are you telling me this now?!" Maddison said mad to her mom. "In the summer you turned 18, and when you turn 18 your powers will start to work." Celeste said. "This is a dream, this is not real." Maddison kept repeating to herself. "This is not a dream." Celeste said. Maddison started to blink with her eyes, Celeste was right, it wasn't a dream.

"Now tell me who attacked you." Celeste said. Maddison did not wanna say his name. "I can't tell." Maddison said. "Alright then, but never talk to him again or even look at him, vampires are monsters and are the worst creatures ever excist!" Celeste said. "Why do you hate vampires so much mom?" Maddison asked her mom.

"Vampire and witches are enemies of each other, and always have been, it all started in 1664, the vampires started to attack the witches, because of us they are vampires, the vampires say its a curse but it was their choice tho, and since that moment, they are the biggest enemies of each other." Celeste explained to Maddison."But why did the witches turned them into vampires?" Maddison asked confused.

"Because they wanted someone immortal, so the witches tried every spell that they could and some how it worked, even tho.. The spell was too powerful, that the witches who did the spell died because is was that strong." Celeste explained to Maddison

"Mom, they murdered Amelia." Maddison said. "They what?!" Celeste said shocked, and Maddison burst into tears into her mothers arms. "They are monsters." Celeste said. "I cannot be a witch, thats just.. unreal." Maddison said. "Welcome to the world of surprises." Celeste said.

"Then what kind of witch are you mom?" Maddison asked and she quickly wiped her tears. "I am a forest witch, they are not that strong as blood witches, so thats why I am telling you this now, you have to watch out, because your powers are developing." Celeste said. "Yeah I will watch out from now on." Maddison said and she went upstairs, Maddison was so tired that she fell asleep at once.

2017 september 7

Maddison woke up and slept well, she hasn't slept while in a long time, she wanted to go trough the day and try to forget about Amelia's death. She was still traumatized about it tho. A little later she was ready for the day and went to school.

(1 hour later) Maddison was sitting in class, Amelia was supposed to be sitting next to her, but that wasn't the case. Jay had told everyone that Amelia was attacked by an animal and died from the wounds, but the thing is that Maddison will be the only person who knows the truth.

"Everyone listen! Today we are going to make a project that has to be finished next week, and you have to do the project in pairs." The teacher said. 'Can I go with Celina?" Some random girl said. "I will choose the pairs." The teacher said. The entire class was disappointed, so was Maddison. "First duo .. Celina and Joseph!" The teacher said.

Celina walked up to the teacher and said, "You will listen to me now, I will not be a duo with Joseph. I will be a duo with Carmen, got it?" And of course Celina was compelling the teacher. "I will do what you say.. Celina and Carmen are a duo!" The teacher said while being compelled.

"Alright next duo, Jay and..... Maddison!" The teacher said. "No you can't do that!" Maddison said to the teacher. "Well I actually can, alright next duo!" The teacher said. Maddison did not want to be a duo with Jay after what happened, Jay did not respond or even showed an emotion. Maddison looked at Jay, but he did not look back.

A little later is was lunch break, Maddison had no where to sit, she usually sat with Amelia. "Attention, Attention! Everyone to the auditorium now! I repeat, Everyone to the auditorium now!" Said the headmistress through a speaker. Everyone went to the auditorium, nobody knew why we had to go there, But Maddison already knew why, it was because of Amelia.

5 minutes later everyone had arrived at the auditorium, everyone was talking with each other, Maddison had actually no one to talk to, Amelia was her only friend. Jay and Celina were standing together, they acted innocent but we all know who killed Amelia. a random girl walked up to Maddison "Hey,

I'm Carmen, I am a bit new here." The random girl said (Carmen)

"Oh hey nice to meet you, I'm Maddison. You can also call me Maddy as a nickname." Maddison said to Carmen. "Alright Maddy! Do you know why we have to be here?" Carmen asked. Maddison wanted to act innocent because she already knew why they had to be here.

"No clue." Maddison said to Carmen. "Attention Attention, everyone quiet and listen please!" The headmistress said. "I think everyone is confused and want to know why we all have to be here." The headmistress said. "Yesterday something very bad happened, Jay and Celina came up to me and told me there was a dead body, I didn't believe it but I still followed Celina and Jay, and there I saw the dead body of Amelia Valencia, attacked by an animal." The head mistress said.

Everyone was so shocked. "Bullshit." Maddison said. "Excuse me Maddison can you repeat that?" The head mistress said to Maddison. Everyone was looking at Maddison, she felt no shame. "Didn't you hear me? I said that it is bullshit, Amelia was not attacked my an animal!" Maddison said angry to the headmistress.

Jay and Celina were looking at Maddison angry. "Then why did she had a bite in her neck from an animal Maddy?" Celina asked to Maddison. "Because you- I mean..Sorry for interrupting ma'am." Maddison said, she couldn't say that Celina did it, because she would get in big trouble.

"I want everyone to light a candle for Amelia." The headmistress said. Everyone walked up to the table where the candles were, they all took a candle and lighted it. Some people were crying, some people did to even knew who Amelia was. "Wasn't Amelia your best friend?" Carmen asked to Maddison. "Yeah, she was." Maddison said to Carmen.

"She seemed like a very nice person." Carmen said. "She could be nice sometime, but when she passed away we still had a argument about something and I regret that I did not had said sorry earlier." Maddison said to Carmen. "Its not your fault." Carmen said to Maddison.

A little later it was already fifth period. Maddison was in English class, and of course Jay was there too. "Alright children, open your book on page 55, and make the assignments." The English teacher said. Jay was raising his hand. "Yes Jay?" Said to English teacher to Jay.

"Can I sit next to Maddison?" Jay said. "Hmm sure, no one is sitting next to her so go ahead." The English teacher said. Maddison did not want that he was going to sit next to her, she wondered why he wanted to sit next to her.

"Hey Maddy." Jay said to Maddison. "Oh shut up Jay, why do you even want to sit next to me." Maddison said to Jay. "There was an empty seat, so I thought.. I am going to sit next to Maddy." Jay said to Maddison. "It was a bad choice, I don't like you Jay and I never will." Maddison said to Jay annoyed. "We'll see." Jay said and Maddison rolled her eyes.

"By the way, wanna work on the project after school? " Jay asked to Maddison. "Your kidding right?" Maddison said to Jay. "Actually I'm not." Jay said to Maddison. "Well I think you already know the answer Jay." Maddison said. "Alright, see you at 3 pm" Jay said to Maddison, and the bell rang, Maddison already knew that she was not gonna make that project with him.

(2 hours later) It was 3pm, Jay was waiting for Maddison to come to the classroom to work on the project, Maddison was hesitant to go to Jay to work on the project, she walked to the class room where Jay was, she opened the door and there was no one. she looked behind her and she saw Jay standing there. "I knew you would come." Jay said.

"Can you stop being behind me all the time? It's annoying and creepy." Maddison said annoyed. "Yeah yeah whatever princess." Jay said and they both walked to their seats. "Alright, let's get this project over with." Maddison said. "Let's do something else." Jay said. "Look buddy, i came here for this project, not to do something fun with you." Maddison said to Jay. "Boooringg." Jay said. "Its sad i can't compel you, if i could we did something fun now." Jay said to Maddison

"Alright, let's do truth or dare if your THAT bored." Maddison said to Jay. "I go first, truth or dare Maddy?" Jay asked Maddison. "Truth." Maddison said. "Do you.. think i'm handsome?" Jay asked. Maddison started to laugh. "You handsome?! I think you need a doctor." Maddison said, but we all knew that that is the biggest lie Maddison ever said, she kept staring at Jay, his ocean blue eyes were shining so bright, it matched perfectly with his black hair. "Than why do you keep staring at me with that look?" Jay asked.

"Because your eyes are so beautiful.. I MEAN NO! THEYRE NOT!" Maddison said accidentally. Jay laughed at her. "Okay my turn!" Maddison said, and when she said that Jay started to look strange at her. "Why are you looking at me like that?" Maddison asked. Jay looked at her confused and said "Why are your eyes red?"

Chapter 5

2017 september 7

"Why are your eyes red?" Jay said confused to Maddison, she looked in the camera of her laptop. "Oh sh*t." Maddison said while she was panicking. "I have to go." Maddison said, and she wants to leave the classroom. But Jay followed her, Maddison turned her back. "Tell me what is wrong." Jay said to Maddison. "Nothing." Maddison said. "Tell me!" Jay said shouting. "No!" and the lights started flashing. Maddison was breathing heavily.

"Did you just do this?" Jay asked. "I-i don't k-know what your talking about." Maddison said and she turned around and walked away, but Jay followed her. "You know what i'm talking about, the lights were flashing." Jay said to Maddison. "Must be a power outage." Maddison said, but she knew exactly why the lights were flashing, it was because of her powers.

"Your eyes were red i'm not that stupid." Jay said. "Well as i said, you clearly need a doctor, it's getting that bad." Maddison said to Jay, she tried to walk as fast as she can to get away from him, she remembered what her mother said, vampires and witches are the biggest enemies of each other, what if he was going to kill her and that he secretly knew that she was a witch, not even a witch but a blood witch.

Maddison turned around to Jay "We are enemies. got it?" Maddison said to Jay clearly. "Since when?" Jay asked to Maddison. "Since now, leave me alone, what part of that don't you understand." Maddison said mad to Jay, she tried to walk as fast as she can to ignore him, but he kept following her, she pulled the door handle to get out of school, Jay was standing in front of the door and Maddison slammed the door right in front of him.

A little later she was almost home, all that walking got Maddison exhausted. Jay was no more following Maddison, she had no idea where he was now.

Maddison finally arrived home, she knocked on the door, she had no keys with her. Celeste opened the door, "What took you so long to get home?" Celeste asked Maddison. "Long story." Maddison said and she stepped inside.

Maddison wanted to walk upstairs but she heard a door knock, who could that be? "I'll open it." Celeste said, she grabbed the door handle and opened the door. "Maddison who is this?" Celeste said confused. Maddison looked at the person standing at the door. "Jay?!" Maddison said.

"The one and only, let me introduce myself miss Delores, i'm Maddison's friend, actually her study buddy." Jay said to Celeste. "I know you from somewhere." Celeste said suspiciously. "Is that so? I don't think i ever saw you." Jay said to Celeste.

"Can i come in?" Jay asked. "Can he, Maddison?" Celeste asked Maddison. "Yea, he can come in." Maddison said and she looked at Jay immediately. "How kind of you Maddy." Jay said to her stepped inside. "So wanna go study upstairs in your room?" Jay asked to Maddison, she looked at him strange and wondered why he is even knocking on Maddison's door, how does he even know where she lives.

"Come on then." Maddison said and they both walked upstairs. "Wonderful house study buddy." Jay said. "Yeah yeah, quit the act Jay, what are you doing here." Maddison asked to Jay and they both walked in Maddison room. "To study with you." Jay said to Maddison.

"You mean so you can study how to know where people live? Cause i don't know what your doing here and why you were following me but just stop with it!" Maddison said, and her eyes were red again, glowing dark red.

"I think you have to calm down, your eyes are red again." Jay said while he was staring at Maddison's glowing red eyes.

Maddison looked in the mirror. "No no i don't want this, it can't be happening this early." Maddison said to herself. "What do you mean that it cannot be happening this early? What are you hiding from me." Jay said to Maddison.

"Nothing." Maddison said. "What are you hiding from me?!" Jay said mad. "I SAID NOTHING!" Maddison said and her powers threw Jay against the wall.

"Oh sh*t." Maddison said. Jay got up with pain in his back. "Your a witch." Jay said with an angry look. "No no it's not what it looks like." Maddison said.

"That's why i couldn't compel you, right?" Jay said. "Maybe." Maddison said. "What kind of witch are you." Jay asked. Maddison looked at him and didn't wanna say it. "That's for you to find out." Maddison said to Jay. "You must be a weak witch then." Jay said to Maddison. "Weak? Didn't you just flew to the wall?" Said Maddison.

"You can't even control your powers." Jay said. "Witches and Vampires are enemies of each other, so that means that you have to stay away from me, got it?" Maddison said clearly. "Who says we're supposed to be enemies?" Jay said.

"My mom does." Maddison said. "And you think that your mom says the truth?" Jay asked Maddison. "I do, she taught me that you guys are monsters, and maybe she's right." Maddison said, but she didn't really meant that. "Then you must be scared of me." Jay said teasing.

"Mhm so scared." Maddison said sarcastically. And they both heated a door knock on Maddison door. "Can i come in?" Celeste asked. Jay and Maddison looked at each other and fast grabbed a book from school so that she saw they were studying. Celeste grabbed the door handle and came in. "Your a Mendez aren't you." Celeste asked Jay. "I am." Jay said to Celeste. "Out of my house." Celeste said mad to Jay. "What no? why?" Maddison asked confused. "I said out of my house!" Celeste shouted to Jay. "Alright then." Jay said and he sighed.

Maddison was so confused. Why was Celeste so mad? Jay did nothing to her, or that's what she thought. Jay walked to the front door and grabbed the door handle. "Wait!" Maddison said to Jay, He turned around and looked at Maddison. "See you at school tomorrow?" Maddison said to Jay, he nodded yes and closed the door. "You are never gonna hangout with him ever again!" Celeste said mad to Maddison. "What did he even do to you then?!" Maddison said to Celeste. "That's none of your business! Now go eat dinner!" Celeste said mad to Maddison.

She was so confused why her mother acted this weird, what did he do to her? Or what did she do to him? She had no clue. Maddison went to the dinner table, her mother already ate dinner.

Maddison sat on she chair and started eating her food, she heard Celeste making a call with someone. "So your coming? We have a huge problem, they're back again in town." Celeste said on the phone. Maddison wondered who it was. Celeste hung up the phone. "Mom who was that on the phone?" Maddison asked Celeste.

"That's none of your business, go eat dinner your food is getting cold." Celeste said to Maddison. Why was Celeste acting so suspicious and weird? Maddison had no idea, maybe her mother was keeping a secret from her.

Maddison walked upstairs, she already finished her food. Her eyes were not red anymore. She brushed her teeth and went to bed, it was late.

The next day..

2017 september 8

It was 1 pm, Maddison sat in class, she looked around but Jay was no where to be found, even tho he said he would come. Maddison looked around if maybe Jays sister (Celina) was at school, but she wasn't. There was no Mendez today, she didn't had Jays number to text him. So the only way was to go to his house.

Why was Maddison so worried about a boy? Not even a boy but a vampire. She had no clue, he drives her crazy, it's like he's in her mind, or she was just thinking that, but if her mother finds out she has gone to his house, her mother would get crazy mad, but Maddison had no fears of her mother, so she decided to go to his house to see what is going on, she knew a bit where he lived so she asked a classmate.

"Hey carmen, weird question but do you know where Jay lives? I have to bring him some papers for our project." Maddison said to Carmen. "Yeah i live next to him actually, it's on the riverside." Carmen said to Maddison. "Alright, thank you." Maddison said and she waited until her classes were over.

1 hour later..

Finally Maddison's classes were over and it was time to go to his house, she had to walk because she didn't had a drivers license yet.

It was 10 minutes later, she finally arrived at his house, Maddison looked around, his house was so creepy, it reminded her of those halloween houses. She looked in the window to see if anyone was home, but the lights were off.

Maddison knocked on the door, the dust and the spiderwebs hang on the door, disgusting. No one was opening the door, she decided to knock again. And still there was no one who opened.

Maddison didn't wanted to wait any longer and decided to get home. It was 15 minutes walk from Jays house to Maddison's house. (15 minutes later) Maddison grabbed the keys out of her pocket and opened the door. "Mom i'm home!" Maddison shouted. "Oh hey sweety, how was school?" Celeste asked Maddison. "Yeah could be better." Maddison said. "So you did not hang around that stupid boy?" Celeste asked Maddison.

"No i didn't mom." Maddison said. But she did texted him, and has gone to his house. Celeste and Maddison both heard a door knock. "Finally there she is." Celeste said. "I'll open the door." Maddison said to Celeste, she grabbed the door handle and opened the door.

Maddison looked with wide open eyes to the person who was standing at the door. The person standing at the door looked at Maddison and said. "Hello sister."

Chapter 6

2017 september 8

"Hello sister." Maddison looked at her sister "Chelsea, why are you here." Said Maddison to Chelsea. "Aren't you supposed to say that you missed me?" Chelsea said to Maddison.

Maddison looked her in the eye and started laughing. "Miss you? Can't you just go back where you belong." Maddison said annoyed. "Maddison! Behave to your twin sister!" Celeste said to Maddison mad. "You can put the word twin away, we look nothing alike not even a bit." Said Maddison.

"Ouch, that hurt." Chelsea said Sarcastically to Maddison. "Why are you even here in Las Vegas?!" Maddison said to Chelsea. "Well i have two reasons, number one is that mom asked me to help you with your powers." Chelsea said.

"Excuse me? I don't need a single help from you." Said Maddison mad. "Reason number two is that we have to help mom get the vampires out of town, they're back again right mom?" Chelsea said and she looked at Celeste.

"Yeah they are." Celeste said. Maddison looked confused and immediately thought of Jay. What if they were gonna kill Jay, but how tho? They're immortal right thought Maddison "Who are the vampires?" Maddison asked to Celeste and Chelsea. Her mom (Celeste) looked at Maddison. "You know exactly who i'm talking about, the Mendez family has to die."

Maddison looked with wide open eyes. "And you will help us kill them." Chelsea said to Maddison. "What..?" Maddison said nervously. "Are you deaf? You my little twin sister will help us kill your friends, and yes i know that he was here yesterday." Chelsea said to Maddison

"What are you my stalker now? I'm not gonna kill them." Maddison said. "If you won't, we will take all your powers, and trust me that will hurt." Chelsea said. Maddison looked at Celeste. "Are you really gonna do this mom?" Maddison said to Celeste.

Celeste looked at Maddison and nodded yes. Maddison was so disappointed in her mom. And she just hated her sister that much that she could even kill her. Maddison's eyes were getting red. "Is my little sister mad? Do we have to calm do down?" Chelsea said sarcastically.

Maddison ran upstairs to her room from anger. She grabbed her phone. She tried to search Jays number, she looked on snapchat and she founded Celina's number. "You have to leave town and get as far away as you can." Maddison texted to Celina.

Celina got online and texted back "Is this some sick joke?" Celina texted back. "It isn't, you have to listen to me i'm trying to help you and Jay." Maddison texted back. Celina didn't reply and blocked Maddison number.

A few minutes later Maddison was done trying to find his number. She just couldn't find it. But then she got a message from a unknown number. "So you tried to find my number?"

Maddison looked at the message Jay send her. "I did, I even came to your house but you weren't there." Jay was typing and immediately sent a message back. "Why? How do you even know where I live?"

"That doesn't matter, the point is that you have leave town, my mother is gonna kill you." Maddison typed back. "What is your mothers name, her full name." Jay sent back. "Her name is Celeste Delores, why? " Maddison typed back. "Are you sure that's your mothers name?" Jay sent back.

"What do you mean? "Maddison typed to Jay. "Because I recognize her from somewhere." Jay typed back but Maddison got offline because Chelsea was knocking on her door.

Maddison walked to the door of her room and grabbed the door handle, she opened the door and saw Chelsea standing there. "What do you want." Maddison asked to Chelsea. "Give me your phone." Chelsea said back. "What? Of course not." Maddison said back to Chelsea.

"I have to check your phone." Chelsea said to Maddison. "Why? " Maddison said back. "To make sure you don't have your cute boyfriend in your contacts." Chelsea said back. "First of all, you're nothing getting my phone, and second of all is that I'm not even friends with him." Maddison said to Chelsea.

"If I find out that your hanging out with him or even talking to him, then your powers.. Are mine." Chelsea said to Maddison and she left her room.

-Jay and Celina's house-

Celina went to Jays room and opened the door. "I got this stupid message from that idiot." Celina said to Jay and she showed the message to him. "You mean Maddison?" Jay asked Celina and she nodded yes. "She is back I think." Jay said to Celina.

"She can't be back, she's supposed to be at the witches forest where she belongs." Celina said back. "If it is really her then that means that Maddison is in danger." Jay said to Celina. "Why would she be in danger?" Celina asked.

"Because Maddison is a witch and her powers just started working, and if her mother is really her then she would take Maddison's powers and that will kill Maddison." Jay said to Celina.

"What kind of witch is Maddison?" Celina asked Jay. "She won't tell me." Jay said back. "She probably is a forest witch just like her." Celina said to Jay. "Well she can't be a blood witch, there hasn't been one since 1876, and they are too powerful even that powerful that they can destroy the whole world." Said Jay to Celina.

"How did you even find out that she was a blood witch?" Celina asked Jay. "She pushes me to the wall with her powers, not on purpose tho. And also her eyes were red." Jay said to Celina. "Only blood witches have red eyes." Celina said to Jay

"And what about fire witches then?" Jay said to Celina. "They have fire eyes, like a orange-red color." Celina said to Jay. "I can't really remember what color exactly it was tho." Jay said to Celina. "Then I guess we will never know." Celina said to Jay

-The Delores's house-

Maddison sat in her room, it was 11pm, she actually should go asleep but she wasn't tired, she was worried about Jay. "See you tomorrow at school." Jay sent to Maddison, she looked at her phone and saw she got a message. "See you tomorrow." Maddison typed back and a little later she fell asleep.

2017 september 9

Maddison woke up and got out of bed, she went downstairs and saw Chelsea and Celeste sitting at the table. "You are not going to school." Celeste said to Maddison. "Since now." Chelsea said to Maddison. "We are doing this so that you will stay away from him." Celeste said to Maddison.

"And I will go to school instead to get him in our trap." Chelsea said. "Oh yeah and by the way, when you were asleep I took your phone so that you can have no contact with him." Chelsea said to Maddison.

Maddison had no words to say, she just was hopeless. "You know, they say that vampires are monsters but you two are the biggest monsters in the whole universe." Maddison said mad to Chelsea and Celeste. Maddison went upstairs to her room, she had no phone, she had nothing.

In the meantime, Chelsea went to school, with Maddison phone. Chelsea unlocked Maddison's phone and saw Jays and Maddison texts.

"Hey jay, its me Maddison. I just wanted to tell you that you suck and I don't want anything to do with you, your bullsh*t. Bye xoxo." Chelsea sent Jay with Maddison's number. Chelsea arrived at school and looked at her class schedule. She went to the classroom where she had to be.

Everyone already sat in class, Jay was waiting for Maddison but she wasn't there. Jay didn't saw the message yet. "Alright children, we have a new student joining us. You can introduce yourself if you want." The teacher said to Chelsea.

"Well what a pleasure meeting you all, my name is Chelsea and I'm so grateful joining this school." Chelsea said while she was trying to act innocent. "You can sit next to Jay Mendez." The teacher said to Chelsea. She walked to the seat next to Jay.

Jay looked at the Message what Maddison sent him, or actually what Chelsea sent him. Jay looked at the message with a confused face. Chelsea looked at Jay and saw he was reading the message. "Oh hey nice to meet you Jay." Chelsea said to Jay. "Oh hey, you're Chelsea right?" Jay said to Chelsea.

"Yeah, I am Chelsea Delores." Jay looked with a confused face at Chelsea. "Are you Maddison's sister?" Jay asked Chelsea. "That's right, I am." Chelsea said back. "I just got a message from Maddison, she's probably mad at me I guess." Jay said to Chelsea. "Maybe she got her period." Chelsea said back and they both laughed. Chelsea tried to get him in her trap.

"Im really bad at math, you seem like a smart boy, wanna help me after school?" Chelsea asked Jay. "Oh yeah sure I guess." Jay said back.

-After school-

Jay and Chelsea were both walking to her house. "So got any siblings?" Chelsea asked Jay. "Yeah I do, I have a sister." Jay said to Chelsea. "She must be nice." Chelsea said to Jay. "Is Maddison home?" Jay asked to Chelsea. "Yeah, why?" Chelsea asked Jay. "I have to talk to her." Jay said to Chelsea. "Oh wait! I forgot, she is on this camp trip or something, so that means she isn't home!" Chelsea said while she was lying.

Jay didn't reply back and they arrived at her home. Maddison looked trough the window and saw Chelsea and Jay walking together. "You got to be kidding me." Maddison said.

Maddison opened the door. Jay looked at her with a strange face. "So she is home." Jay said. "Oh yeah I forgot, the trip was tomorrow, silly me!" Chelsea said. Celeste walked to the door and saw Jay standing there. Celeste looked at Jay and said, "Its time."

Chapter 7

2017 september 8

"Its time." Jay looked confused at Celeste. "What do you mean w-" And he was given an anesthetic in his neck and he fell on the ground. "Jay!" Maddison said and she bent down to the ground where Jay lay. "Wake up Jay!" Maddison said but he did not woke up. "We expect that not us will kill him, but you Maddy." Chelsea said to Maddison.

"I- i can't." Maddison said. "You know what's gonna happen if you don't." Celeste said to Maddison, she started thinking. If Maddison didn't kill him, her powers would be taken away and that would kill her, she had no choice. Maddison looked at her mom and Chelsea and said, "Okay I'll do it."

"That took long for you to say." Chelsea said to Maddison. "And how do you wanna kill him..?" Maddison asked. "With a wooden stake, that's how you kill vampires." Celeste said. "You have to stake them trough the hart." Chelsea said. "Teleport him to the basement mom." Chelsea said to Celeste.

Celeste bent to the ground to hold Jay's hand, and in one blink they were gone. Chelsea went to the basement and Maddison followed her. They went to a secret room where Jay was locked up. Chelsea looked at Maddison and opened the door of the room where Jay was locked up, Celeste went out of the room.

"Here's the stake." Chelsea said to Maddison and she pushes her into the room and locked the door. "What are you doing?! Why are you locking me up?!" Maddison yelled mad.

"You can only get out if you kill him, if he isn't dead tomorrow then you know what is gonna happen." Celeste said to Maddison and they both went upstairs. "Im fooled." Maddison said to herself, she looked at Jay who was still unconscious. "Jay wake up!" Maddison said to him.

Jay finally woke up and slowly opened his eyes. "Maddison?" Jay said. "Finally you woke up." Maddison said to Jay. "You tricked me, you locked me up in this trap!" Jay yelled at Maddison. "No no, I swear I didn't want this to happen." Maddison said to Jay. "And that message?" Jay said. "What message?" Maddison said confused.

"Don't act dumb Maddison, you send me a message that I was bullsh*t." Jay said to Maddison. "I didn't send that, my sister took my phone probably and send it to you." Maddison explained to Jay.

"My sister lured you in their trap." Maddison said to Jay. "And now what are you gonna do to me? Kill me?" Jay said to Maddison. "I-i don't know, I don't have a choice." Maddison said while she was holding the stake in her hand.

"Put that stake away Maddison." Jay said. "I can't." Maddison said and Jay grabbed the stake out of her hand and pointed it to her. "Your too weak to kill me, on who's side are you." Jay said while he was pointing the stake to Maddison. "I don't have a choice okay?! You just don't get it!" Maddison said to Jay mad. "What do you mean with that you don't have a choice, of course you do." Jay said to Maddison.

"My mom and my sister are gonna take my powers from me." Maddison said to Jay. "That will kill you." Jay said to Maddison and she nodded yes. "A mother wouldn't do that." Jay said to Maddison, she had no reaction. It all suddenly made sense to Jay, he let go of the stake and stepped back.

"You have to escape Jay, I can't kill you." Maddison said. "We will escape both." Jay said. "How?" Maddison asked. "Use your powers." Jay said to Maddison. "I can't control them." Maddison said. "You only have to think, just use your brain and teleport to my house." Jay said. "Hold my hand and do it." Jay said to Maddison.

Maddison held his hand and tried to use her powers. "You can do this, come on." Jay said to her. Maddison eyes were turning red and she tried to teleport, she used every energy of her body to teleport, Maddison wanted to look at Jay and he was gone. Only Jay teleported. "Sh*t." Maddison said to herself.

Chelsea came downstairs and saw that Jay was gone. "Explain Maddy, where is he." Chelsea said to Maddison. "I killed him, but then his body just teleported because my powers couldn't control it." Maddison said lying. "So he is dead?" Chelsea asked, Maddison nodded yes.

Chelsea opened the door of the room, Maddison walked to Chelsea and whispered in her ear, "A little secret, I teleported him when he was still alive." And Maddison pushed Chelsea to the wall with her powers and quickly locked the door. "You b*tch." Chelsea said and Maddison ran upstairs.

"Mom I got him, Jay is dead go look." Maddison said to her mom and Celeste walked downstairs to go look, while Celeste was looking if he was dead, Maddison ran to the front door to escape from her home before they could kill her, she ran as far away as she could.

In the meantime Celeste went to the basement to see if Jay was really dead, Celeste took a look and saw Chelsea standing in the locked up room. "She betrayed us!" Chelsea said mad. Celeste unlocked the door and opened it. "Where is Jay." Celeste said. "Maddison teleported him away when he was still alive with her powers and locked me up in here." Chelsea said to Celeste.

Celeste's eyes started to turn dark green, the forest witches eyes. Celeste went upstairs "MADDISON WHERE ARE YOU!"

Celeste shouted angry. She saw that the front door was open. "That little brat ran away." Celeste said. "We have to find her and kill her and the boy."

In the meantime Maddison was still running as far away as she could, she had no phone and no home, she was homeless at this point. She saw Jays house from a distance and ran to it. Maddison was exhausted, she knocked on his door hoping he would be there. Jay opened the door, "Come in fast before they see you." Jay said to her and he grabbed her hand to go to his room.

"How did you escape?" Jay asked Maddison. "I said i killed you and Chelsea let me out, then i pushed her into the room and locked her up and went upstairs to tell mom that i killed you, she took a look to see if it was true and i ran away, as far as i could." Maddison said to him.

"But the thing is that I'm homeless now." Maddison said to Jay. "You can live here." Jay said to Maddison. "No I can't do that, this is your home I can't stay here." Maddison said to him. "You will stay here Maddison, I will not let you be homeless." Jay said to her.

Celina opened the door of Jay's room. "How did you get here Jay? I was supposed to go home with you, and what I she doing here?" Said Celina.

"Long story, the thing is that Maddison is going to live here." Jay said to Celina. "What?! Nah that's not gonna happen."

Celina said. "She is in danger, and actually.. We all are in danger Celina." Jay said to her. "Me in danger?" Celina said confused.

"Maddison's mom will kill us all, me and Maddison were locked up a half-hour ago." Jay said. "Jay, what if it is really her.." Celina said to Jay. "It could make sense." Jay said. Maddison was confused about what Celina said. "What do you mean with that?" Maddison said to Celina.

"What was your mothers name again Maddy?" Celina asked. "Celeste Delores." Maddison answered back. "And she's a witch right?" Celina asked and Maddison nodded yes confused. "What kind of witch?" Celina asked. "Why all these questions?" Maddison asked. "We just have to know, just answer them Maddison." Jay said.

"She is a forest witch, and my sister is a fire witch, happy now for knowing?" Maddison said. "It just doesn't make sense." Jay said to Celina. "Im confused, what doesn't make sense what are you guys talking about?" Maddison said confused. "We are talking about Katherine Valés, never heard the evil stories about her?" Celina said to Maddison.

"I did, when I was little. My sister used to tell them to creep me out, but she isn't real right?" Maddison said to them. "She is, Katherine did many bad things to us." Celina said back. "Like what things..?" Maddison asked. "That's none of your business." Celina said to Maddison. "Oh so first you wanna interview me and now it's none of my business?" Maddison said mad to her.

"You are just so dramatic Maddy." Celina said to her, and Maddison's eyes started glowing red. "Your a blood witch.. It isn't possible." Celina said. "They haven't existed in years." Jay said.

And Maddison's eyes stopped turning red. "You have to look out with your powers Maddison, just in one click you can destroy the world." Jay said to her. "Ive been told that the whole week now." Maddison said and she rolled her eyes.

"Im gonna head to my room, I'm pretty tired from all this talking." Celina said and she left Jays room. "Im gonna go downstairs get some food, call if you need me or if there's something bothering you, alright?" Jay said to Maddison. "Yeah I will." Maddison said and Jay went downstairs.

Maddison looked around his room and saw pictures of him and Celina, she took a look and saw pictures of them when they were little, Jay's room was so mysterious, it was all with dark colors.

Maddison heard someone calling Jay one the phone, his phone was still on his desk. It was a unknown number, who could that be? Maddison picked up the phone. "Hello? Who is this?" Maddison said on the phone. "Tried escaping? Bad choice."

Chapter 8

2017 september 8

"Tried escaping? Bad choice." The person said on the phone. Maddison was breathing heavily, "Chelsea you don't have to do this." Maddison said on the phone. "This isn't Chelsea." The person on the phone said. "Then Who is this?!" Maddison said on the phone questioning, but the person hang up the phone.

Jay came upstairs to his room where Maddison was, she had his phone in her hands. Jay looked at Maddison. "You probably like my background on my phone, you may keep staring at it." Jay said to Maddison and winked sarcastically.

"No its not that, there was someone calling you." Maddison said to Jay. "Who called me?" Jay asked. "It was a unknown number so i decided to answer the phone while you were downstairs, but the person said on the phone that escaping was a bad choice, i thought that it was Chelsea but the person on the phone said that she wasn't her." Maddison said stressed.

"We're screwed." Maddison said hopeless. "We aren't screwed, we just need to find a plan to get away from them, we can't run away forever." Jay said to Maddison. "Yeah but we can't go to school." Said Maddison while she was thinking deeply for a plan.

"If we go to school, they would find us there."

"Exactly." Maddison said.

"Or... We have to end them." Jay said to her, she saw the words coming out of his mouth and it was repeating slowly In her mind. Maddison couldn't end her family. Even tho they wanted to end her. They didn't care about Maddison, even tho she is their family.

Maddison was staring at Jay, like a dead stare. Her mind was in another universe it seemed like, her mouth was slowly repeating about what Jay said. "Maddy?" Jay said confused while he looked at her repeating the words she kept saying.

Maddison stopped staring and looked at Jay. "Wha- NO!" Maddison said frustrated. "Im not going to kill my own family." Maddison said. There was a dead silence after Maddison said that. Jay didn't answer, Maddison didn't say something. They were both deeply thinking what they could do.

It was like a murderer was going to kill them. Jay walked out the room without saying anything, it was like he was mad, mad about being complete hopeless. Maddison was still thinking.

Maddison grabbed Jay's phone and unlocked it, she knew that Chelsea had Maddison's phone. Was Maddison ready for it? Was she ready to call Chelsea? She wasn't. But she still did it.

she clicked on the icon to call her, she was actually calling herself, but she knew Chelsea had her phone after all. The sound of the ringtone went off, she hoped that Jay would not know this or hear the ringtone at all.

After 10 seconds Chelsea answered the phone. "Meet me in 20 minutes at cemetery square." Maddison said on the phone and she hung up quickly before Chelsea could even say a word.

Maddison didn't wanted that Jay or Celina would know that she was gone for a while. So she was as quiet as a mouse walking downstairs, making sure Jay didn't see her, he was in the kitchen looking for something, Maddison wanted to know what he was doing but she didn't want to be conspicuous.

Step by step she walked to the front door, took the handle from the door and tried to open it quietly without making a sound. Maddison stepped outside and closed the door quietly.

Maddison heard someone looking out the window, it was Celina, she opened the door of her window and saw Maddison standing there. "What are you doing? You shouldn't go outside or you'll lure them here." Celina shouted to Maddison. "SSHH!"

Celina looked confused at Maddison. "Jay can't know! Please don't tell him!" Maddison shouted to Celina. "What? I don't g-, you know what I'll see you later, bye bye Maddy." Celina said to her and she slammed the door of her window.

Maddison took a deep breath and starting to walk to the cemetery square hoping Jay would not find out.

-15 minutes later-

Maddison finally arrived at the cemetery square and saw Chelsea standing there, she came. "Finally, that took you long. You said 20 minutes and it took you 23 minutes. That means you're late." Said Chelsea.

"Im not here to fight, okay? I think we just have to..Sort things out." Maddison said in a nervous way. "What are you now some fairy godmother who thinks she can be kind?" Chelsea said in a angry way. Maddison didn't answer on that. "You really don't get it do you?" Chelsea said to her. Maddison looked confused at her and said, "What do I don't get?"

"You took my shine! Everything you took away from me with just one click in your fingers! It all started when she told be that you were a blood witch, at that moment i meant nothing to her anymore, she was only busy with you. Your powers meant so much to her. All the attention she gave to me just was gone in one blink. And it's only because you're a blood witch." Chelsea said angry, all of that just came out of her mouth at once, anger, betrayal, Chelsea all fell it.

"Now I understand it, your jealous of me, jealous of that I am a blood witch and that you are not." Maddison said to her, it suddenly all made sense to her.

"But finally mom realized what kind of a brat you actually are, finally I replaced you, I even have your room now isn't that crazy?!" Chelsea said evil. Maddison didn't knew if she just was born evil, or it was her powers.

Maddison couldn't be angrier as she was right know, everything what Chelsea said wasn't right to Maddison.

"Everything that just came out of your mouth was a waste of time, stop acting I was the favorite child because you know that I wasn't, who could go on vacation with her alone? You did. Who did she ask to help with her work? She asked you. And most importantly, who did she ask to help her get rid of the Mendez's? It all was you." Maddison said angry.

Chelsea looked at Maddison like she just could murder her in one blink. "You will regret that what you just said." Chelsea said while she was staring at her with a dead stare. "Just leave Jay alone. He did nothing wrong."

"Nothing wrong?! He is a vampire Maddy get that in your damn mind!" Chelsea said to her and grabbed a knife out of her pocket and pointed it to Maddison. "Ive been waiting for this moment, for a long time." Chelsea said to her while pointing the knife. "Put that knife away." Maddison said and she stepped back.

Chelsea got closer to her. Maddison had no one to save her, only her powers.. Maddison looked at her hand and a redness flame came off her hand, were her powers working?

Or not? Maddison tried pointing her hand to Chelsea hoping her powers do something, but they didn't.

"Aren't your powers working? What a shame Maddy." Chelsea said while still holding the knife. "Do it, kill me." Maddison said to her. Chelsea looked confused at her. "Why not beg for your life?" Chelsea asked.

"What's the point of that? Come on, murder me." Maddison said with no shame. Chelsea wanted to step closer to her but they both saw someone waking to them, Maddison looked at the person walking to them. "Jay?!" Maddison said confused.

Jay saw Chelsea holding the knife to Maddison, his eyes started to glow red, dark red. Chelsea had no weapons to protect her from a vampire, no wooden stake. Chelsea wanted to teleport to somewhere else but Jay stopped her, he holds her by the throat and looks her straight in the eye.

"Think you can run now because you can't protect yourself? Bad choice." Jay said to Chelsea holding her throat. "I- I c-can-t bre-ath." Chelsea tried to say, but before Jay knew Chelsea teleported herself.

Jay turned around and looked at Maddison. "Have you lost your damn mind?!" Jay said mad shouting at Maddison. "Sneaking out of the house?! I offered you to stay at my house, to even live there! And this is what I get back? Ungrateful."

"I just thought that maybe I could make her on our side.." Maddison said to him. "Maddy, you have to get one thing clear.

We can't make them on our side, they were born evil." Jay said to her clearly.

"She wanted to kill you Maddison didn't you just saw that?" Jay said to her. Maddison said to reaction back and the scene and Chelsea was holding a knife to her was repeating in her head.

"We're going home." Jay said mad and turned around wanting to walk home, but Maddison was still standing there. "You coming or what?" Jay said to her. Maddison looked at him in the eye. "Mhm." Maddison said and she walked home with him.

Jay was still mad about what Maddison did, when they walked home they haven't said a word to each other.

5 minutes later they finally arrived home. Celina opened the door and looked at them. "Romeo and juliet finally arrived." Celina said sarcastically. "You knew this right? That she would sneak out?" Jay asked Celina mad. "No clue what your talking about." Celina said while trying to act dumb. "Yeah whatever Celin." Jay said while Maddison was following him.

Jay wanted to go to his room alone to calm down about what happened. "Wait Jay." Maddison said to him while he wanted to open his door room. "What." Jay said annoyed.

"I'll do it." Maddison said. Jay looked confused at her. "Do what?" Jay said confused to her. Maddison looked up and down and said, "We'll do it, we will end them."

Chapter 9

2017 september 8

"We'll do it, we will end them." She said. Jay looked at her like she was speaking Chinese. "Wait, are you sure?" Jay asked. "Yes, I am." She said in a way just like she was emotionless.

His expression dulled, "Follow me, I'll show you your room." He said and she followed him. There was an awkward silence, were they both mad at each other? Or was something bothering them?

"Here, feel like you're home." Jay said and he left Maddison in her room, it was an empty room with only a bed. the dust was coming off the walls and it looked old, who would have ever slept here?

Maddison sat on the bed and looked around the room. Who would have thought that the boy who attacked her that night would offer her to live with him in his house? These days were too crazy for Maddison, so much happened in such a short time

1 hour later, it was 10 pm. Maddison was laying on her bed, she looked at the ceiling and so many questions were going trough her head, she was mad at Jay, when he shouted at her she felt like she was a horrible person. Maddison heard footsteps coming to her room. Jay knocked on her door, she didn't answer but Jay still came in.

"Why don't you answer when I knock?" He said. Maddison did not even answer of that. "What's wrong?" He asked. Maddison did not look at him but she just stared at the ceiling. "I'm just tired." She said. "Liar." Jay said. "Is this of because of what happened at the cemetery square?" He asked her, but she said nothing

"Sorry I yelled at you, that wasn't necessary." Jay said quietly. Maddison turned around and looked Jay in the eye.

"Sorry that i did not told you." She said. "Sorry did not hear you." Jay said teasing her. "Yeah yeah funny." She said and he smiled at her. "Nighty night Maddy." He said and he closed the door.

Maddison was trying to get to sleep, and she did. But after a while she woke up, someone stood behind her. Maddison turned her back and saw her mother standing there. "You think you can run from me?" Celeste said. "HELP!" Maddison said. Jay ran to her room and opened the door.

"Maddison!" Jay said. "Wake up maddison your dreaming!" He said. Maddison opened her eyes and was breathing heavily. "S-she was there, my mom!" She said to him frustrated. "Maddy it was a dream, she isn't here." He said to her. "But she was just there."

"They won't find you here Maddy, everything is okay." He said and Maddison got back to sleep.

The next morning...

2017 september 9

Maddison was sleeping deeply after what happened at night. Someone opened her door."Wake up sleeping beauty!!!!" Celina said to Maddison.

Maddison opened her eyes slowly and immediately looked at the time. "It's 7 am!?" Maddison said. "Yeah well, i have a plan because you and Jay are too scared to even fight back." Celina said to her. "You even had this weird nightmare i heard."

"We aren't going to school right?" Maddison said. "Wow, never expected from you to be that stupid, anyway come downstairs in 5 minutes."

"5 minutes??!!" Maddison said back and she immediately got out of bed, the clothes that she was wearing right now were disgustingly, but she didn't had any other clothes to wear, they were at her "old home."

Maddison was walking downstairs and she already saw Celina and Jay sitting at the table. "Took you long enough." Celina said annoyed. "Is she always so annoying?" Maddison asked Jay.

"Anyways, i have a plan, so please listen if you mind." Celina said. Maddison sat at the table with Jay and they both looked at Celina. "So this is the plan, we are going to your house Maddy." Celina said to Jay and Maddison. "Are you stupid?" Jay said to Celina

"We can't go to my house, Chelsea and my mom are there." She said to Celina. "You really think that i was supposed to do that. The thing what i meant was, we are going to they're house when they are not home."

"To do what?" Jay said to her. "They maybe have some secrets that they're hiding, or some plans. You never know." Celina said. "But when do you know when they aren't home?" Maddison asked.

"They are looking for us Maddy, of course they aren't home." Celina said to her. "So when we're going?" Jay said. "Now." Celina said back

Jay grabbed his car keys and they all walk to the door. "Nervous, Maddy?" Celina said. Maddison rolled her eyes and walked to the car.

4 minutes later..

It was quiet, the entire car ride. They finally arrived and Chelsea and Celeste weren't home. "As i said, they aren't home." Celina said proud.

They all got out of the car and walked to the door Maddison had her house keys in her pocket and opened the door, they all looked around the house for things that Chelsea or Celeste were hiding. "Lovely home Maddy." Jay said to her.

Celina was looking in the drawers and saw tons of paper. "Bingo." She said.

There was a note from someone, there was no name on it only an apology, the letter said: "Sorry that i didn't had the time to raise you." That's what the letter said. Celina looked confused and looked for a name on the letter, but she didn't find it.

Celina was looking threw the papers while Maddison was in her room grabbing her stuff, Jay came in her room and looked at her pictures, he saw a picture of that Maddison was little.

"Look at that, you were pretty cute to be honest." Jay said. Maddison looked at the picture. "That's Chelsea, not me." Maddison said. "I mean i was sarcastic." Jay said immediately after that. Maddison laughed at him. "Embarrassed?" She said to him

"By you? Nah." He said to her. Maddison looked at him in the eyes.

Maddison's pov:

I looked at him in the eyes, his blue oceaan eyes. I never saw anyone with that much blue in their eye, but he? He definitely got it. How can you even believe that behind those blue eyes is a devil is disguise, a vampire. I'm not saying that Vampires are Devils, but they have red eyes, right?

What am i even saying? That i like his blue eyes?? No i don't, i don't want to like him. Or do i? I had no clue. Or was i falling in love? NO! I am definitely not.

Mom always said that I don't have to fall in love who you don't trust. Did i trusted him? No clue, i mean he did ask me to live in his house. I actually shouldn't even be listening about what mom always said.

Jay's pov:

I kept looking at Maddison, and she kept looking at me. I don't know why i am so obsessed with her, i never been into girls that much, i've always never cared about love or anything of that actually. She made me feel different, she was special. But do i trust her? I don't know. She is one of the evilest witches of all time tho.

I don't even think that she wouldn't even care if i get hurt because all after what i did to her?! Nah. Even tho i was locked inside her house, but that doesn't matter. I think that Maddison is innocent. Running away from her family, that's pretty tuff.

Maddison had those green eyes, green as grass. And black wavy hair, was it her natural hair? I guess so..

Maddison and Jay were looking at the stuff in Maddison room. Maybe there was something strange in her room? Maddison didn't thought so, she literally lives here, or actually "lived"

Celina was still looking trough the papers, she saw a passport of Celeste, she was looking at the passport but the name on the passport wasn't right. it said Celeste Valéz. Celina looked with wide open eyes. "GUYS!" She shouted.

Maddison and Jay came downstairs and saw Celina standing there with the passport in her hands. "You got something?" Jay asked.

"Look." Celina said, and she showed Jay and Maddison the passport. "This can't be real." Jay said. "Why does it say Valéz? Her last name is Delores.." Said Maddison.

"Let's just go home, and bring the papers with us so that we can look home." Celina said. "Is Celina scared?" Maddison said laughing. "Don't joke about this Maddison, we are going home right now, it isn't safe." Celina said.

Maddison was confused, Jay knew exactly what she was talking about. Celina took all the papers that were in the drawer and wanted to walk to the door, but then they heard a car parking at the house, Chelsea and Celeste were home.

They all looked outside and saw Chelsea and Celeste getting out of the car. " Shit."

Chapter 10

2017 september 9

" Shit." Celina said. They all panicked. "Hide somewhere, quick!"

Maddison ran upstairs to her room, she always had a hiding spot there. "Hide with me." Maddison whispered to Jay. They both ran to Maddison's room as quiet as they could, but they had no idea where Celina was hiding.

Maddison grabbed Jay's arm pulling him towards the hiding spot. "Hiding in a f*cking closet, seriously ?! " Jay said. "What was I supposed to do, hide under the covers?" Maddison replied. Both rolling their eyes at the same time, they suddenly hear the footsteps on the stairs.

Maddison's hands shaking with fear. What if they find me? What will happen? All these questions we're going trough her head. She could feel the fear rising. "Jay I' m scare- " Maddison whispered. Suddenly Jay grabs Maddison's waist spinning her around slowly while his hand covers her mouth. " Sshh she's here." Jay whispers.

Pinned up against him with her back, Maddison's mind races. While her mind is overwhelmed with the thought of being caught the feeling of Jay's presence softens it. Maddison feels at ease knowing Jay Is right behind her, litteraly! Footsteps are getting louder.. faster and Closer! Then suddenly.

There's a dead silence... Maddison closes her eyes in anxiousness while jay is still holding her close. "Oh hello hello!" Maddison' s eyes flash open. That voice... " I know you' re in here, come on out!" Jay can hear Maddison' s heart racing. "I' m not going to waste my time playing hide and seek, I'm going to make you want to come out, you little b*tches!" An evil laugh follows that sentence. Maddison can' t see a thing but she knows. That voice.. That evil laugh..

"It' s Chelsea." Maddison mumbled. Chelsea walks to Maddison's nightstand, picks up a picture frame. Maddison can finally see something. "No, please no." Maddison mumbled again. "Some will think I won't burn this disgusting picture of Maddison and the dead beat dad." Chelsea says.

Maddison tries to wiggle out of Jay' s arms, but she can't move an inch. " Come on you know me of course I will!" Chelsea says playfully. In just one second the picture goes up in flames. The one and only picture of Maddison with her dad, that holds a special place in her heart is gone.

Maddison's knees turn numb, Jay catches her when she is almost about to fall. He can feel the tears streaming down Maddison's cheek. While the picture burns away, Maddison turns her face towards Jay. Jay meets her broken gaze. Staring into her eyes filled with tears, it hurt.

" stay focused Maddy." Jay whispers concerned. "Let this be your warning! I know how to find you and when I do. It's you who I'll burn!" Chelsea screams angry.

After waiting a few minutes, they finally hear the car driving away. Maddison pushes Jay away and runs towards the ashes on the ground. Maddison breathes heavily, anger building up inside her. " How dare she." Maddison says angry.

"Why didn't you do something?!" Maddison says angry to Jay, tears were going down her cheeks, Jay looked at Maddison with no emotion. "You could've done something!" She said angry to him. "Its too late, the picture is gone now." He said.

"You don't even care that the picture burned in flames." She said with tears in her eyes. "I do but what was I supposed to do? We were hiding there for a reason Maddy." Jay said, She wiped the tears from her cheeks. "Go find Celina, I'm going to grab my stuff."

Jay was walking downstairs looking for Celina, while Maddison was still looking at the ashes on the ground, her only picture with her dad. She could do nothing anymore, the picture was already gone just like Jay said.

She picked up the ashes on the ground and put in in the trashcan, she stood up and grabbed a bag to put her stuff in. Maddison saw Jay coming upstairs again. "She's gone." He said with his eyes wide open. "What do you mean she's gone? She has to be here somewhere." Maddison said frustrated.

Jay looked around to see if maybe she was upstairs, but she wasn't. "I LOOKED EVERYWHERE MADDY! SHE IS GONE!"Jay said angry. "Calm down Jay." she said, but he didn't. he looked at the vase on the cupboard and picked it up "Is this vase special here in this house?" he said. "No?.." and he threw it hard against the wall out of anger.

"She is dead Maddy, do you think they are gonna be kind and keep her alive? No." He said frustrated. Maddison held his hand and looked him in the eye. "We still have hope." She said.

"Come on, let's go and find her." She said to him while holding his hand. Jay was still livid, filled with rage. You could easily tell he was about to lose it.

Maddison's POV:

Wow, i never expected Jay to be that protective over his sister. I mean it's good tho, but i've never seen Jay that angry before, but i'll do anything right now to find Celina for him.

I looked at the pieces of the broken vase on the ground, wasn't it moms birthday present when she turned 43? No idea, I didn't even care about my mom at this point actually, i can't even call it a mom anymore, she failed at being a mom to be honest, and Chelsea?! She never felt like a sister, and after burning my picture with my dad, that's where she crossed the line, i would like to call it a war now between us.

The only picture with my dad, he gave me it when i turned 13 years old, and after that he just disappeared, no clue where he is now.

Jay grabbed his car keys, he looked at me like it was over, that he would never find his sister again. But trust me, he would.

Jay and Maddison sat in the car driving, they had no idea where to start looking. "Where could she be." Jay said questioning himself. "Give me your phone." She said to him while looking at the road. "Why?" He asked confused while driving. "Just give it!" And she grabbed his phone.

"Maddy what are you doing?" And he looked at her while he was driving. "Look on the road!" She said scared looking at the road.

"Scared princess?" He said charming. "Just look on the road." She said and she looked at his phone. "What are you doing on my phone if i may ask?" He asked her. "I am going to track Chelsea's location." She said while being busy on the phone.

"Where did you learn that?" He asked. "My dad thought me how do to it." She said and she tracked her location.

"Bingo." She said. "Where are they." Jay said focusing on the road. "West Spring Mountain Road, hurry." She said looking at him. Jay drives as fast as he could to West Spring Mountain Road where they had Celina.

5 minutes later~

"there they are, that's their car!" Maddison said to Jay while she was pointing to their car. Jay drove way faster as he did a few minutes ago. "Crash their car." Maddison said. "Your insane, i'm not gonna do that." He said to her.

" You have to, they won't stop the car so we're gonna do it in my way, crash the damn car Jay." She replied. "The car will explode, it will hurt." He said looking at her. "You will survive it, Celina also, don't mind me. Now, crash. The. F*cking. Car." Maddison said while having red eyes.

Jay didn't wanna do it, he didn't want Maddison to get hurt. But they had no choice, there was no toner way. Jay threw his arm around Maddison and held her tight. "U sure?" He asked and she nodded yes.

Jay drove as fast as he could to the car. the car was almost against Celeste's car, another inch and it touched. "Come on." He said while he was driving with one arm on the steering wheel and one arm around maddison.

Jay's car was going faster, too fast actually. The car finally crashed into Celeste's car, both cars flew into the air causing a big explosion. Everything blew up in the air. Fire catching quick surrounding the place.

Boom. The cars were both in flames. Maddison slowly opens her eyes, she was bleeding. the sharp glass of the car hit deep in her stomach, she breathed deeply in and out, stay focused maddy, she said to herself.

She tried to get up but the pain stopped her, she didn't want Jay to see that she was bleeding, so she took all the strength she had in her body and tried to get out of the car. As hard as it is for Maddison to keep going. She puts her misery aside. This is about getting Celina back.

Jay opened his eyes slowly, he got out of the car and saw Maddison standing there holding onto her wounds. "Get Celina." She said to him while blood kept flowing down her stomach. Jay didn't see that she was holding her stomach or that she was bleeding. Jay saw Celina in the car and they both looked at each other as they both saw Chelsea and Celeste being unconscious.

"Didn't expect you to come." She said while getting out of the car. "Duh, i'm not gonna leave you with these monsters." " you sure chose the extreme way." Celina said. A smile turned on Jay's face " Well it was maddy's idea." He said grabbing her hand helping her to get out of the broken car. "Right, Where actually is Maddison?" Celina asked Jay. "She's standing over there." He replied. Celina looked confused at Maddison, she knew that there was something off.

Jay and Celina walked over to Maddison. "You okay Mads? You don't seem okay." Celina said worried. Jay looked at her stomach. "Your bleeding."

Chapter 11

2017 september 9

"Your bleeding.." Maddison looks back to her stomach then looks back up to the concerned looks of Celina and Jay. Her eyes meeting His eyes. "What's going on?" Maddison said confused. "You're stomach, it's bleeding don't you feel it?" Celina said with a shaky voice. Realisation hits Maddison. " So much blood, i.. i- feel tired." Maddison replied and she almost falls on the ground but Jay catches her.

"No! You need to stay awake." Jay said demanding. Jay rips open Maddison's shirt. "Jay what the actual f*ck." Maddison says. "Sst this is not the time to act tough." Jay said. "Where's my mom and Chelsea??" Maddison asked " They're passed out, don't worry about that. Let me look at your wound." Jay replied.

Maddison groans " It stings." Maddison said. "Your wound is not that deep, but your loosing too much blood. Celina look for something to tie around!" Celina looks around the broken cars seeing if she can find some type of frabric. " I can only see these Two witch bitches laying half dead." Celina called out.

" F*ck, alright keep an eye on them. I' ll take care of maddy." Jay said. Jay rippes open his shirt tying it around Maddison's stomach. " Yes, the bleeding is stopping." Jay said happily. He throws his head back with relief. " Maddy you will be okay, I will never let this happen to you again." Jay says. There was no response from Maddison. "Maddy?" Jay asked confused.

Looking back at her he finally realises maddy's eyes are closed. While being busy stopping the bleeding. Maddison's body is giving up on her. The blood loss is to much.

"Maddy! No no no.." jay said stressed. Shaking Maddison's body she fails to respond . "Open your eyes Maddy. Right now! Don't you dare die in my arms." Jay yelled. Celina comes running over. " J.. ay?" Maddison said tired.

"Oh God, Maddy don't scare me like that." Jay said relieved. " She will pass out again, tie the shirt on her wound tight." Celina said. "Sorry, this will hurt a bit." Jay said to Maddison and he tied the shirt tighter, Maddison screams from pain. "You'll be okay, i promise." He said to her and they all heard someone getting out of the car.

It was Celeste, Maddison looked at her mother with pain from her wound she tried to stand up. "Well well look who has got their karma." Celeste said laughing looking at Maddison. "Oh shut up Cruella." Celina said to annoy her. "You little brat, i almost got you, i can still kill you all in one blink, but that's not part of my plan." Celeste said evil.

"Maddison come with me, i'm your mother." Celeste said to Maddison looking at her. "I think she's safe with us, she doesn't need you." Jay said while holding Maddison's wound looking if it is still bleeding, the bleeding stopped. "You'll regret it Maddison, you all will."

Celeste said to them and she saw Chelsea getting out of the car. "Why did you have to wake up? It was calmer here when you were out of consciousness." Celina said to Chelsea looking at her annoyed.

Chelsea walked over to Celina. "You better watch your mouth you creep." Chelsea said while her eyes meeting Celina's. "Or what?" Celina replied. "Or else i will rip yo-" Chelsea wanted to say but Celina pushed her to the ground. "Whoopsies, my hand slipped." Celina said laughing.

"Does mommy need to help you now to get up?' Celina said annoying Chelsea. "Celina enough." Jay said to her, Celina rolled her eyes. "Pathetic." Celina replied. Maddison stands up with all her strength she had in her body, the wound still hurt. "Look, we don't need to fight." Maddison says looking at Celeste and Chelsea. "We actually do, you chose their side." Celeste says to her.

"We have much plans for you in the future, right mom?" Chelsea said turning her head to Celeste. "The future isn't that much away, prepare for it I would say." Celeste says evil and they teleported in one blink to their home.

"You okay Mads?" Jay said to her turning his head to Maddison. "Yes, I'm fine. Let's just go home." She said tired. "Wait a minute, we're not gonna walk to our house, right?" Says Celina.

"How else do you wanna get home." Jay replied."Ehh." Celina says and she looks at Maddison. "She's not gonna teleport us, she has a stab wound are you blind?" Jay says to Celina.

"I mean i can try?" Maddison says. Jay looks at her "No your not." Jay says serious. "Why not? It can't hurt." Maddison replied. "I will not let you sacrifice yourself again." Jay says to her.

"I can do whatever i want with my powers." Maddison replied. "It's dangerous." Jay says. "You only live once." Maddison says back. "Your powers don't even work." Jay says to her. and he rolled his eyes. "Watch me." Maddison replied and her eyes started to glow red, not even red but dark red.

"Hold my hand." Maddison says to Jay and Celina, they walked over to Maddison and held her hand. "Ready?" Maddison says, they both nod yes.

Maddison closes her eyes and holds their hands tight, and just in one blink they teleported to Jay and Celina's house. "Home sweet home." Celina says and she looks around the house.

"It really worked, didn't expect that to be honest." Jay says to Maddison. "Just had to try it." She replies. "How's your wound?"

He asks Maddison. "It's fine, doesn't hurt that much anymore." Maddison replied. "I'm gonna head to my room, call me if you need anything." He says and he goes upstairs.

2 hours later--

Maddison's POV:

Today was a crazy day, just like every day from now on i guess. I never expected that i would ever get hurt, like a stab wound, luckily i stitched it when i got home, if Jay wasn't there with me, i would've died lonely. I got to say that he cared much about me that moment.

And the papers in the drawer.. What could it mean? It said "Celeste Valéz". Is mom hiding something? I have no clue. But the name reminded me of something, the stories Chelsea used to tell me when i was little about Kathrine Valéz. It made no sense, maybe i am just not thinking straight.

And also about that letter, it said "I'm sorry i didn't raise you" Something like that, i don't really remember what it said exactly but this means something, maybe there were more letters? I had no clue.

Maddison sat in her room, when they teleported she brought her stuff still with her, stuff from home, like clothes and those things. Celina opened the door and came in her room. "Hey roomie." Celina says to her. "Well hey." Maddison replied putting her clothes down. "Soo ehm, thanks i guess for saving me." Celina says awkward. "Never thought that you would say thank you? But no problem i guess." Maddison says looking at her.

There was a awkward silence. "Alllrightt. This is getting cringe in gonna head out." Celina says and she wants to leave the room. "No wait." Maddison says and Celina turns around facing Maddison. "You still got those papers?" She asked Celina. "I do, I haven't looked if there was more in it, i'll grab them wait right here." She replies and she walks to her room to grab the papers.

"Got them." Celina says and she sits on Maddison's bed. "Let's see what we got here." Celina says and she looks trough the papers and she sees Maddison's passport trough the papers, she grabs her passport and looks at it. "Maddy explain this, why does this also say Maddison Valéz?" Celina asks her confused.

Maddison walks over to the papers and looks at the passport. "It doesn't make sense." Maddison says while looking trough the papers. "That we're all the papers i brought here." Celina says.

"These papers mean something important i think, or maybe it's just some crab Chelsea ever made to prank me." She says. "Who knows." Celina says and she grabs the papers and walks over to her room.

Jay's POV-

Today was crazy, i was scared that i would loose her. When i saw that my girl got hurt, there was a spark in me that was lost for years, but it just came back, emotion.

When i heard Maddison's scream as i tightened my shirt around her wound tighter, i was terrified. That scream was too painful to even hear. And after i heard that scream i knew that i would never let her get hurt ever again.

Celeste and Chelsea were those ugly b*tches just like those two sisters from the movie cinderella. How dare they even want to hurt Maddison, only because she chose the good side, i could tell that it is insane.

Everyone was in their room, thinking of what happened today, but then the doorbell rang, they all walked downstairs and fast as they could. "Who is it?" Maddison asked. "Only one way to find out." Celina says and she grabs the door handle and opens the door. "Carmen?" Maddison's says confused looking at her.

It was Carmen from school, Celina Madison and Jay had a few classes with her. But the moment when they looked at Carmen, she was covered in blood. "Please help me, they are after me."

Chapter 12

2017 september 9

"Please help me, they are after me." Carmen said exhausted and with tears in her eyes. "Who is?" Celina asked confused looking at the blood dripping on Carmen's clothes.

"C-celeste and Chelsea." Carmen said scared. They all looked confused at Carmen, why would Celeste and Chelsea want to attack her?

"come inside and tell us what happened." Maddison says and Carmen wants to come in. "No way, this isn't a f*cking hotel." Jay said angry, Maddison looks at Jay,

"Come on Jay, i'm not saying she gets to stay here but i just want to know what happened." Maddison says to him. Somehow Jay just can't say no to Maddison. Jay let's out a deep sigh "Fine." He says and Carmen enters the house.

They all sit on the couch and everyone is looking at Carmen. "By the way don't get my couch dirty with that blood on your shirt." Celina says to her and she looks disgusted. "Alright tell us what happened." Maddison says and she leans on the couch.

"So i was walking down the street, Chelsea said to me that she wanted to make homework with me, so i walked over to her house."

"I knocked on Chelsea's door and her mom Celeste opened, she grabbed me by my shirt and she asked me if i was friends with Maddison, i was scared I just nodded yes."

"And then she says to me that she wants me to kill you Maddison, i said no because why would i kill someone? but then she started threatening me, she said that if i won't kill you, she would burn the whole school down."

"I don't want her to burn the whole school down, but i'm also not going to kill Maddison, she told me the story what Maddison did, and how she betrayed Celeste and Chelsea, and when i heard the story i knew that i wasn't safe. So i ran." Carmen said.

They all looked at Carmen in awe "And why did you ran to my house?" Jay asked Carmen. "Because i thought that you guys would help me out." Carmen replied.

"Why didn't you ran to your parents house? It's not like that we can solve your problems." Jay says to her. "I live alone, my parents left this country for their work." She says.

"And i forgot to tell, Celeste and Chelsea also just burned my house down." She said troubled

Jay, Celina and Maddison looked at each other, what are they going to do? "Give us a moment." Jay says and they all walk to the kitchen so Carmen couldn't hear them.

"What are we supposed to do?" Celina says anxious. "She is homeless!" Maddison says."I don't even know her, and i bet that she will be begging to stay here." Jay says annoyed.

"Maddison had the same problem, and you offered her to even live here, so what's the big deal? She seems alright." Celina says. " That's different" jay replies fast. "Anyway your saying you want me to offer Carmen to live here?" Jay asks annoyed. "Actually, yeah. It's our house so that doesn't mean that you can decide everything." Celina replies pissed.

"You know what Celina, if you want her to live here so badly then why don't you let her sleep in your bed?" Jay says annoyed. "You'd probably lo-" Celina wanted to say but she couldn't finish her sentence because Carmen came in the kitchen.

"Sorry, i didn't mean to interrupt but.. i also have a brother, i can't leave him all alone in the street so i think im gonna go-" Carmen says and she walks to the door. "Wait!" Jay yelled. Carmen turns her head facing Jay. "Fine, you can stay here with your brother until Chelsea and Celeste are dead" Jay says and Maddison looks at him. Again it hits her. sometimes she forgets that she has to kill her own family.

"Where is your brother exactly?" Celina asks. "I just called him to come over." Carmen says.

"Yeah anyways, Celina show their room when her brother gets here." Jay says and he rolled his eyes, he walked upstairs and he slammed his door.

"What has gotten into him." Maddison says. "He's acting like a girl who just got her period." Celina says and Maddison chuckled at her joke.

They hear a doorbell ringing. "That must be my brother!" Carmen says and she opens the door.

Maddison's POV:

I had no bad feeling about that Carmen and her brother would live here, the house is pretty big so it doesn't mind that much, but when Carmen opened the door their stood a tall boy, brown hair, hazel eyes.

He started to look directly at me. His look was so.. mysterious as i could tell. He looked at me like this wasn't the first time we met.

I would sometimes meet him in the school hall but we never talked that much, Carmen was new at school, but he was pretty known there.

"Hey James." Carmen says to him, Celina and Maddison were looking at James. "Hello ladies, thank you so much for offering us to stay here, we really appreciate it." He says friendly.

"Yeah no problem, i'll show you both your room, you both will have to share the room." Celina says to them and she leads them to their room. "There you go." Celina says and she closed the door when they came in the room.

2 HOURS LATER -

It was 8pm, they all ate dinner and all sat in their room, but something wasn't right. Maddison's mind was racing. She was stressing. Then suddenly she heard a knock on the door.

"Come in!" She says. The door opened as she saw James coming in. "James right?" She asks him. "That's right Maddy." He says to her with a smile on his face. Why would James call Maddison "Maddy" She didn't even knew him that well to have a nickname.

James sat on her bed sitting next to her, it was getting awkward. James kept getting closer to her. Maddison was breathing heavily, as soon as she looked at him he placed his hand on her knee. "I'm sure you don't mind me calling you Maddy." James said charming. " Ehh, Yeah no problem." She said awkwardly.

Maddison's POV:

Why was i getting nervous? And why was he sitting this close?!! My breath was so heavy right now. His hand on my knee, why is he touching me? Too many questions. He probably does it at everyone he knows, some boys are like that, right? I looked at him awkwardly and nervous.

He kept giving me this look, a strangely but also friendly look, i don't know what he was exactly trying to do, but it was suspicious as you could tell. Jay hasn't seen James yet, he is been sitting in his room for hours.

"So Carmen told me everything, she also told me that your a blood witch am i right?" James asks her. "Yup, that's right. And Jay and Celina are vampires." Maddison says to him. "Yeah, she told me that as well."

"How is your wound?" He said to Maddison and he switched his hand on maddison's leg. "How do you know i have a wound?.." Maddison's asks strange.

"Well Carmen told me kinda everything as she heard from Celeste, let me look at your wound." He said and he pulled Maddison's shirt up touching her. But Jay came in Maddison's room."Don't touch her." Jay says while looking directly at James.

The directing comment from jay shook both me and James out of our moment. The tension in this room is definitely rising. Maddison looks at jay but.. jay isn't looking at her. No he is looking directly at James. Giving him a dead stare. Maddison takes a quick look at James. She can't read what he is thinking is he scared or angry. She looks back at jay. Now Suddenly jay looks straight in Maddison's eyes. Not in a nice way, he seems annoyed even disappointed, why??

Maddison is startled. Is he that mad about him touching me?! "Get out" Jay says demanding. " Excuse me ?!" Maddison replies. Jay rolls his eyes. "Not you Maddy- You." Jay says while fixing his gaze on James.

Chapter 13

2017 september 9

"Not you Maddy- You." Jay says while fixing his gaze on James. "What's up with the attitude bro?!" James says. Maddison realises that this pushed jay over the edge. Because .. His eyes turned glowing red. " I give you a f*cking place to sleep, I offer to help you and your sister. And you have the nerve to question me." Jay says with no emotion. It's scary how calm but crazy he is. "Get the f*ck out punk." Jay yells. James gets up walks up to jay. " Take it easy bro, it was only a touch." James whispers in jay's ear. Jays fist clenches while James walks out the room.

Maddison looked at him angry, not just angry but furious. "Are you out of your f*cking mind? First you ignore us all and now this?!" Maddison yelled angry. "He touched you."He replied while yelling at her. "So what? Are you jealous?"

"You wish." He said mad and after that sentence they both stared at each other, there was a dead silence. Jay walks out of the room slamming the door right in front of her face. Maddison was fuming at this point, so mad that her eyes started to glow.

Her eyes changed into a red colour, not just any red. It was a deep dark red. While her eyes were glowingFlames came off Maddison's hands, she is in some sort of trance, a shock. She doesn't realise everything that is happening to her. Suddenly every light in the house started flashing wildly. Maddison looked around wondering what's going on. Thinking it's just an power outage, she finally picks up on what is happening. Her hands radiating flames that are as hot as the sun yet she doesn't feel a thing. She stares.. stares at the huge flames on her hand getting bigger, brighter and wilder.. More out of control.

And then suddenly.. Celina comes in her room. "Hey i jus- .. " Celina stops speaking when she sees what's going on.. "Oh my gosh Maddison.." she says in awe."Uhm are you okay?" Celina asked carefully. Maddison's eyes express how angry she is, the red flames resembles her fury. While Celina is still trying to talk to Maddison, she doesn't get a response. Maddison is overwhelmed trying to gain control, she doesn't take in what Celina is saying. Maddison is breathing heavily. The beautiful vase that stood in her room exploded into tiny pieces. Celina got startled by the explosion, lost in what to do..

Jay came running to her room. "What was that?!" He said, then he saw Maddison standing in her room with those dark red eyes. Maddison looked at Jay angry, she just couldn't control her powers.

"Go away Jay." She said looking at him. "I think you should calm down." He replied, he walked closer to her trying to be as careful as he can. He knew that her powers could be dangerous. "Go away!" Maddison screams. Jay gets thrown up against the wall letting out a groan of pain. Celina couldn't believe it.

Maddison's eyes stopped being red and the flames on her hands were gone, "Shit." She said running towards Jay. "Sorry! I didn't mean to.. i mean-" She says "It's fine, I got my karma i guess." He said getting up.

"No its my fault." She says to him. "It isn't, don't say that." He says looking at her. "You should get rest." He says to her. "I will, goodnight Jay." She says to him ' Night Princess." Jay said

Maddison's POV

Did he just call me princess after I launched him up against the wall.. or am I really tripping!? I can't even control my own powers.. it's like a curse. Whenever I want to use my powers they just become more than I can handle. The amount of power I feel within me is overwhelming and I really need to gain that control. I don't want to hurt anyone especially.. jay. F*ck I feel so bad I lost it in front of him. And not just that. I hurt him..

When my powers start to show I feel like a monster.. like I'm one of.. them. They say all blood withes are dangerous , but if I can learn to be different than them? I can be good, right? Man i have no clue. So many questions are going trough my head at the same time.

I was still thinking about the papers, the notes, and the weird phone call, the papers.. i just didn't get it, why would there be such papers in the drawer about something i never knew about? It didn't make sense.. All i know for sure is that this isn't right, i should better get to sleep, it's been a long and intense day.

2017 september 10

The next day..

Everyone was already awake, it was 9am. Maddison was still asleep, suddenly she heard yelling from downstairs. She opened her eyes slowly and immediately got out of bed. Her hair was a mess, she walked around with those silly pink pyjama's and head over downstairs. As soon as she looked at them, it wasn't yelling, they were watching soccer, and yelled of happiness because their favorite team scored.

"Morning." Carmen says to Maddison. "Morning." She replied and goes sitting on a chair. The rest of them were watching soccer expect for Carmen and Maddison.

Maddison looks at Jay, he is focused on the soccer game on tv. Maddison walked up to Jay who was sitting on the couch watching the game, she tapped on his shoulder and looked at him "Can we talk?" She asks.

"Sure, one second." He said, he grabbed his phone putting it in his pocket and got up as he followed Maddison to her room, he closed the door and Maddison stood right in front of him.

"Alright, what did you wanna talk about." He says . "I just have a gut feeling about the papers." She says to him looking in his eyes she quickly looks back to the ground. "What about it." He says confused. "Well, you know what the papers says, i think it's about me. And i wanna find it out." She says looking back at him. "We can't spend every day stressing about papers and running away for Celeste and Chelsea." He says crossing his arms. "I know but it's not that we're free to live happy." She replied.

"I'm not gonna run away forever, not again." He says, Maddison looks confused at him, what did he ment with "again" ?

"What do you mean?" she asks. "Nothing." He says, he wants to walk out of her room but Maddison grabbed his hand. "Are you hiding something?" She asks holding is hand. He turns his head towards her looking in her eyes "No." He says and he lets go of her hand. Maddison let out a deep sigh. What was he hiding? And why was he acting this way?

Maddison quickly stopped caring about that because her priority now is finding out what those papers mean, if she wants something, she's making sure she gets it. She started thinking of that one phone call, it said something with "bad choice".. She needs to call that number, but one problem. It's on jays phone and he really isn't giving it to her. He thinks it's a bunch of bullsh*t. So there is only one way to get to jays phone. It's time to steal.

"Well, if your done daydreaming, I'm gonna go." Jay says snapping Maddison back to reality. Damn I forgot he was here. Jay starts walking towards the door. "Wait!" Maddison says stopping jay from leaving. " I just wanted to thank you for how cool you've been about last night." Maddison says while thinking of a way to steal his phone from his pocket. "Yeah no problem." Jay replies." "And not just that.. I want to thank you for everything you've done for me." Maddison says while moving closer to jay. What the actual am I doing-

"Where is all of this coming from." Jay says confused. Maddison grabs his shirt pulling him towards her. " I'm just lucky to have you.." Maddison's says. Jay looks at her intrigued on what she is up to. "And I like having you close to me.." Maddison whispers. "I'm going to kill myself after this." Maddison thinks. Jay is suprised on how bold she is. Jay moves his mouth closer to hers. Maddison is regretting putting her self in this position. "Damn this man know how to tur- Snap back at it!" Maddison thinks. Now's the time.. aha I got the phone. Maddison has what she was out for but- she can't help but feel like she is taking advantage of Jay. "How come your so outspoken today?" Jay asks.. "I.. I just-"

GOALLLLL!!!! The loud cheering broke jay and Maddison apart. Thank goodness " Maddison says under her breath. Jay takes a step back. " I'm going back to watch the game." Jay says. "Alrighty." Maddison replies. Jay walks out the room. "Alrighty" seriously Maddy. Well atleast I have what I needed.

Maddison first grabbed the papers out of her drawer and began to search the note. Seeing if there was a name on it, but the only thing she saw on it was a "K" in the corner of the paper. What could this meant? Who's name started with a K?

Now it's time to check the call. luckily she knew the password of Jay's phone, she unlocks his phone and goes to his calls, she sees the unknown number.

Does she have the confidence to call the number, Maddison was scared, what if they would track her location. Stop it Maddison, your thinking too much, she thought.

She wants to click the icon to call the unknown number, but something flies trough her window, a note...

She walks to her window trying to reach the note as it falls on the ground, she picks it up and starts reading. -I'll be back today.- is what is written on the paper. "What the..?"

Chapter 14

2017 september 10

"What the-" Maddison said looking at the note confused, what could this mean? There was nothing more on the note, on that sentence. She was brainstorming, she just couldn't believe it, "What the f*ck is that." Jay said standing in her room, Maddison didn't even realize that Jay was standing there this entire time. She turned her head facing Jay, She stood up fast and put the note behind her so that Jay didn't see it. "Nothing!" She said awkwardly. "What are you hiding?" He asks her confused. "Just like i said, nothing." She says to him. Jay sees his phone laying on the ground. "Hey- Is that my phone?" He says confused and quickly picks the phone up laying on the ground. "Why do you have my phone." He asks but she doesn't know what to say.

"It must have fell out your pocket." She says looking at him with dull eyes. "Mhm sure." He says and wants to walk out of the room. "Wait! Okay i'm sorry, i took it because i want to find out stuff and i didn't want you to find out, i thought you would get mad."

He took a deep breath, "Glad your being honest." He says and Maddison came closer, "I have to say something." He says. "Go on."

"I uhm, look. We've been sleeping in the same house for a few days and every time i look at you then you just drive me crazy."

Maddison looks at him with wide open eyes, she has no reaction.

Maddison's POV

Is he being honest? The way he looks at me is also driving me crazy, what is he even trying to say with this?

Every time i look at him, the only thing what i see in front of me is a perfect man, perfect face, perfect eyes.

"I like you." He says. "From the beginning i attacked you that night, i knew i couldn't take my eyes of you, you've been in my head since that night every second and i can't stop thinking about you."

"Really?" She asks, "Yes Maddison, really." Maddison came closer to his mouth and so did he, they're lips felt each other

Maddison's POV

I melted into his arms, taking the graceful sensation of his touch, as i grasped the back of his neck. His hands, gentle yet possessive, cupped my face with a tenderness that took my breath away.

As our kiss deepened, I lost myself in the intoxicating feel of it all. Each brush of his lips against mine sent sparks of electricity trough me, which made me wish that this moment would never end.

2 Months later-

It was two months later and nothing changed much, Carmen and i got a good friendship together, So did James with Jay,

Me and Jay after that one kiss, everything was perfect. We didn't even cared about Chelsea and Celeste anymore, it was like they just disappeared. And about that one note, it must have been a prank, that's what my hopes wanted.

We've been to the club, got drunk, watched the sunset together. Me and Jay were in love if i had to be honest, life was perfect at this moment, nothing could go wrong.

"Jay! I'm gonna order pizza! Who wants some?" James shouted, everyone came downstairs and all said what they wanted to order. 20 minutes had past and the pizza delivery was finally there. "I'll get the door." Maddison Says

As she walks to the door, she grabs the doorhandle and opens the door, she saw a strange lady with green eyes, black wavy hair, with no pizza in her hands. "So, where's the pizza?" Maddison says confused. The woman kept staring at Maddison like she hasn't seen her in ages. "I'm so glad your okay my daughter."

Chapter 15

2017 november 10

"I'm so glad your okay, my daughter" The lady said to Maddison.

She looks confused at the Lady. "I think you got the wrong house." Maddison says and she wants to close the door but the Lady holds the door open. "It's me Maddison." The lady says to her. "Your scaring me."

"What is taking so long-" Jay says and he walks to the door facing the lady. "Maddison get behind me." Jay says to her. "What why, what's going on?" Maddison says. "Katherine Valéz." Jay says.

"What?! Katherine Valéz isn't real." Maddison says to him. "She should tell by herself i think, right Kath?" Jay says angry getting red eyes.

"Still the old Vampire as you were i see." The lady says and she chuckles. "Maddison, can we talk?" The lady says. "No way." Jay says for her. "It's fine Jay, it will be just a few seconds." Maddison says and she steps outside and closes the door.

"Maddison i'm so sorry for leaving you with her, i had no choice." The lady says. "What..?" Maddison says confused. "Let me explain this, Celeste isn't your mother, she is my sister."

"I've been put in prison world, i've done bad things, but now i'm just like you Maddison."

"This must be a joke." Maddison says. "It isn't. The note i tried to sent you, i couldn't come on that moment, but i'm finally here now. Face to face i see my daughter safe."

Maddison couldn't believe it, all this time Celeste lied to her. "And what about Chelsea?" She asks.

"That isn't your sister, we've put a spell on her to make her look like you so that you would believe that she is your sister, i couldn't take care of you in the past because i was put in prison world with other blood witches, so i asked my sister Celeste to take care of you."

"So, your a blood witch?..." Maddison asks carefully. "I am, i have a house with all "our" people, blood witches. Come with me Maddison, we can be powerful."

"No thanks, I will stay here. It's safer.." Maddison says and she steps inside. Wait, here's my number if you change your mind." The lady says "Katherine".

Katherine took out a note with ur phone number and gave it to Maddison. As she closed the door Jay stood right in front of her. Maddison was still shocked, Celeste wasn't her mother? And chelsea wasn't her sister?

"Don't ever talk to her again." Jay says to her and places his hand on Maddisons shoulder. "Jay, she is my mother, celeste was never my real mother, she's her sister." She says to him.

Jays mood switched immediately, "What.." Jay says confused. "I don't get it why you hate her." She asks him. Jay looks mad, angrier than ever. And getting red eyes. "SHE KILLED MY PARENTS!"

"And then you have the nerve to tell me that she is your mother?!" Jay says having deep red eyes coming closer to Maddison as she steps back. "Getting involved with you was the worst mistake i ever made."

Maddison looks at him with betrayal. "

"You don't mean that." "I sure do, you are a mistake Maddison." "Stop." "Stop what? Your just like her Maddison, it's in your blood."

Maddison walks upstairs mad, real angry. Maddison took all her stuff upstairs in a bag and wanted to teleport out of this house, this house was a mess right now for both of them. As she teleported out of the house, she took her phone out of her pocket and called the number Katherine gave her. "I'm coming with you."

Chapter 16

2017 november 10

"I'm coming with you." Maddison says on the phone. "Teleport to me." Katherine says and she hangs up. As Maddison teleports to Katherine she sees a massive cave. She starts walking in the cave and it was cold and dark in the cave, at the end of the cave she sees lights, and more lights.

As she looks more she sees a big door, she knocks on the door and Katherine opens it. "Welcome home daughter." She says to Maddison and leads her into the blood witches cave. "This is massive." Maddison says looking around, she saw more blood witches training on their powers, you clearly saw that Katherine was their leader.

"Ladies and gentleman! we've got a new member." Katherine shouted and everyone came to her. "This is Maddison Valéz, my daughter. We will be more powerful with her in our team to Kill the vampires." Katherine says to them.

Maddison didn't care anymore, she didn't even had a choice anymore, it wasn't like she wanted to kill Jay or Celina, but she wanted to be away from them.

She looks at the people surrounding around her. Her eyes landed on two people who she recognized, she looks more and better and she sees Celeste and Chelsea standing there.

What are they doing here? Is this why we didn't heard from them? "Celeste and Chelsea, i heard you wanted to kill my daughter?" Katherine asks them. They both don't respond. "I'm done with you sis." Katherine says. "Send them to prison world!" Katherine says to the blood witches.

Maddison looks with wide open eyes while they were doing the spell to send them to prison world. And just in one second they were gone. It was like they never where here.

"Now everyone go train your powers! Maddy i'll show your room." Katherine says, Maddison and Katherine walked up to her room, their were many other rooms for many people as she saw. "Feel home sweety, call me if you need me." Katherine says and she leaves maddison in her room. She looks around the room, it was bigger than the one in Jays house. a luxury bed, tons of closets.

Mendez house-

"Jay, Have you seen maddy?" Celina asks him. He doesn't answer. "I'm talking to you!" Celina shouted in his ear. "I don't care where she is." Jay says angry. "Romeo and juliet got into a fight?"

"She's Katherine's fucking daughter." Jay says mad. "W-what?"

"You heard me, she belongs to them." Jay says. "But we sent her to prison world?." Celina says slowly "We did but she found a way to get out."

"Maddison is gone." Carmen says shocked. "She's what?!" Jay says angry and he storms upstairs to her room breaking the door open. "She's at katherine, she chose her fucking side. Jay says angry. "We're going to kill Katherine AND Maddison." Jay says to Them.

Chapter 17

2018 February 10
3 months later-
Maddison's POV

Rise and fucking shine, 3 months had past and i was more powerful than ever i would say, i could control my powers, i don't get it why the fuck they said it was dangerous, because it isn't. I even learned how to fight like a real woman.

I can't wait anymore to Kill those bastards, vampires. Especially Jay, i didn't gave a fuck anymore about him, his change is gone. He means nothing to me anymore. I don't understand what i ever fucking saw in him.

I became a different person, not so pathetic anymore, the people here learned me that i don't have to care about people who don't care about you. My powers made my emotions better, it was like they were gone.

I knew that today we would attack the vampires, or the vampires would attack us. And i would see that fucker again. Jay, Celina, Carmen, all pathetic little bitches. Celeste and Chelsea were still in prison world, no sign of them.

Me and my mom talked about a lot of stuff, i still can't believe she ever killed Jay and Celina's parents, she was too good for that. She says that her powers overtook her. But they betrayed us all, vampires were monsters.

Jay POV-

3 months had past and no signal of Maddison, it was not like i care but one thing i knew was that it is war between vampires and witches, me and Celina learned carmen and James about fighting, so that they can fight back when they attack.

Katherine has killed my family in the past, and then she wanted to kill us but we managed to escape and me and Celina ran forever.

We teamed up with more vampires, more of our people to destroy them.

"Attention everyone, today is the day. IT IS WAR!" Katherine yelled at everyone. Now it was time, the day they all waited for. "We're teleporting in a few minutes to the vampires!"!Katherine shouted, everyone stood by katherine, so did maddison. Everyone was ready to teleport, and so they did. "TELEPORT NOW!"

In one blink they were at a vampire house, a house with all vampires. This is where Jay brought his people together.

Everyone ran to the door and in one blink the door broke in to tiny pieces. from now on it was war.

Everyone was fighting with each other, spells, powers, vampire fangs, and especially red eyes everywhere. Maddison was killing every vampire one by one. She turned around to kill more but she was directly facing Jay. They both looked at each other with no emotion. "Maddison." Jay says to her covered in blood of killing witches. "The pathetic little bastard showed up." Maddison says. "You've changed." He says to her.

"No shit." Maddison says. "What are you waiting for punk. come on, Fight." Maddison says and she punched him in the face multiple times, she used her powers and started to choke him with red flames coming of her hands, her powers were too powerful as Jay saw.

Jay kicks her in her chest trying to stop her powers. Maddison kicks him to the ground. "Tired already?" Maddison says and she chuckles evil. She wants to punch him again but someone puts their hands on her mouth. "Don't make a sound." Celina says wrapping her hands around her mouth so she can't speak. Celina takes a syringe from her pocket and sticks it in maddison's neck and she fell to the ground being unconscious.

Jay grabs her body laying on the ground and celina is making sure no one sees him. He exists the house walking to the car where James and Carmen were waiting. He places her body in the backseat and locks her up. "Drive. " Jay says to james who was driving.

2 minutes later-

"So, how did it go?" Carmen asked them. "I don't even recognize Maddison anymore, it's like her powers are controlling her." Jay answers. "She's hurt." Celina says.

-10 minutes later they arrived at Mendez house.

Jay walked while holding Maddison's body to the basement where he put her on a chair and tied her up. A little later she finally woke up. Her head was spinning and everything was dizzy.

Jay was sitting in front of her watching her while she woke up. "What the fuck, where am i." Maddison says while being dizzy. "The basement."

"Your embarrassing Jay." She says mad. "I get that your mad but we can fix thi-

"No way in hell." She says. "Let go of your powers." Jay says carefully. "No thanks." Maddison says chuckling. "Your powers, It's killing you, don't you see it?" He says. Maddison doesn't say anything.

Jay's POV

The only way to get her back is to show up emotion. I have to get my girl back. Just like Celina said, i hurt her. Her powers are killing her and it's my fault, but i'm going to fix this.

Jay walks up upstairs to get Celina. "I need a little help sis." Jay says to Celina. They both walk downstairs to the basement. Celina looks at Maddison and sees that she is completely lost. "Can't handle me on your own? Sad." Maddison says.

"Maddy, i'm sorry okay?" "You don't know how much i regret it that i spoke to you that day, it's the biggest mistake i ever made, i was in love with you and i just ruined it." Jay says. Maddison looks at him and her eyes stopped being red. "I love you Maddy."

"You don't mean that." Maddison replied. "I do. I love you Maddison, please forgive me." He says. "I love you too."

Jay quickly untied her and they both deepened in their kiss. "Ew, you know i'm still here right?" Celina says while breaking their moment. "Oh forgot that." Maddison says. "Glad your back Mads." Celina says walking towards her hugging Maddison. "I'm glad aswell." Maddison says.

1 hour later-

One hour later and Maddison got her old room back, she talked to Carmen and James and everything was normal between them. But after a few minutes they all heard a big gun shot coming from the backyard, Celina Jay and Maddison both ran to the backyard to see was happened, as they looked good, they saw James and Carmen being dead on the ground with a note on their head. They were all mad, who could've done this? They were innocent. Maddison grabbed the note who was laying on the ground beside their body. "This is for choosing their side Maddison, xoxo katherine." Maddison says reading the note. "Were going to kill Katherine .. Today." Maddison says mad.

Chapter 18

2018 February 10

They all were training for the final battle Maddison was angry at Katherine for murdering Carmen and James, everyone was angry to be honest. Maddison had control over her powers in a good way. Her emotion was back.

Maddison's PoV

I am going to make an end to katherine, i finally realized that she manipulated me all this time, she lied to me. She used me to be powerful. But we have a plan to kill those blood witches.

We're going to put a bomb into the cave and hopefully it will kill most of the blood witches. Hopefully it will kill my mom, my real mom this time.

"Come on, it's time to kill those monsters." Celina said to Jay and Maddison as she walks to the the car, the bomb was already in the car. The only thing they had to do is place it in the cave and press one button.

5 minutes later-

Jay was driving the car and Maddison and Celina were in the backseat talking with each other.

They finally arrived at the cave and they all got out of the car as they walked to the massive opening of the cave. They placed the big bomb at the door and all ran to a different place to get as far away from the bomb. "Ready?" Jay said and Celina and Maddison both nodded yes as Jay pressed the button to explode the bomb.

A massive explosion came from the cave, and many blood witches got hurt. After a few minutes the fire from the explosion was over and the people who survived came out of the cave and saw Maddison Jay and Celina standing over there.

Katherine came out of the cave covered in blood, she walked over to maddison with a few people who survived the explosion. "pathetic standing over here." Katherine says to them. "It's pathetic your still alive." Celina replied. "I'll kill you Celina, don't think you can run away this time." Katherine says evil. "I won't, this time i'll make sure there's a end to this." Celina replied.

"Let the battle begin."

As the battle ensued, magic crackled in the air as spells were cast. The sound of cries and screams filled the night as the two sides fought with all their might. Celina moved with lightning speed, dispatching witches left and right with her deadly grace.

Jay prowled like a predator, using his vampire powers to take down any who dared to stand in his way.

Maddison found herself torn between her loyalties, but ultimately chose to stand with Jay and Celina fighting against her own kind. She used her blood magic to shield her allies and strike down the witches who sought to harm them. Despite the chaos and bloodshed, Maddison felt a sense of peace knowing that she was fighting for what she believed was right.

As the battle raged on, the casualties mounted on both sides. The once powerful blood witches fell one by one, Jay Celina Maddison covered in blood. Most of the witches had an stake to kill vampires. When Maddison faced Katherine they both looked at each other deep in their red eyes."I'll give you one last change Maddison, come with me we can be powerful." Katherine says to her. "Never again, you manipulator."

After that sentence Katherine got mad and choked Maddison with her powers. She couldn't breath. Celina saw Maddison get choked and kicked Katherine to the ground.

Katherine quickly stood up and she pulled a wooden stake out of her pocket. Celina wasn't scared for a wooden stake and kept punching Katherine.

As she kept punching, Katherine stuck the wooden stake into Celina's heart and she fell on the ground. "NO!" Jay screamed running towards Celina's body laying on the ground. Jay hold her hands "Don't let me die Jay." Celina said while Jay was pulling the stake out of her heart. "Your not going to die here celina." Jay said hoping that pulling the stake out of her heart would help, but it didn't. Celina's eyes were open and she didn't blink. "CELINA!" Jay screamed pushing her body hoping she would still be alive, but she didn't wake up anymore.

"NO! CELINA WAKE UP!" Jay screamed, he looks at katherine and getting red eyes with vampire fangs. "Your so dead." He said grabbing a knife who was laying on the ground.

Jay ripped open Katherine's neck and kept stabbing her many times. Maddison watched him stabbing her multiple times, he didn't stop. "Jay she's dead."

"Stop Jay she's dead." Maddison says. "She's still here so she clearly isn't." Jay said while stabbing Katherine with the knife. After a few moments he finally stopped and he took a deep breath. "My sister is gone." He said.

Maddison looked at Celina's body with tears in her eyes. "She tried to save me." Maddison says.

"She told me to not let her die, i failed." Jay said looking at her body. "It's katherine's fault." Maddison said and she turned her head to say if they killed everyone.

But they didn't, there was still one person alive hiding with a gun in his hands. "You sure we killed everyone?" Maddison asked. Jay looks around but sees with his red eyes someone hiding behind the trees holding the gun in his hand pointing it to maddison. "MADDISON WATCH OUT!" Jay screams. But it was too late, the bullet was going right trough maddison's head. "MADDISON!"

Chapter 19

2018 February 10

1 hour later-

Maddison's POV

The last thing i remember is someone shooting a bullet in my head, i slowly opened my eyes. Where was i? I was in a room, a bedroom. But no one was there. I quickly stood up. I've never seen this bedroom before. The only thing i focused myself on was the mirror. As i walked to the mirror i looked at my face. My eyes were a different color red. Deep red. I felt something hurting my mouth, i opened my mouth and i saw vampire fangs.

"You finally woke up." Jay says walking towards her. "I thought i lost you too." Jay says."W-what's going on, my eyes, my tooth." She says confused shaking with fear. "This isn't real, they shot a bullet trough my head." She says looking in the mirror with

Jay standing behind her. "You did die, but i found a way to save you."

"I turned you into a vampire Maddy." He says to her looking at her vampire fangs. Maddison was breathing heavily. "Your a blood witch and a vampire now." Jay says.

"That isn't possible." She says confused. "A blood witch combined never happened before, they call it the Blood empire." He says.

"I'll learn you everything about vampires, but first we have a funeral to go to." He says and letting out a deep sigh.

2 hours later-

As they arrived at the small funeral home, Jay and Maddison were the only ones in attendance for Celina's funeral. Despite the empty room, Jay knew that he needed to say a heartfelt speech to honor his sister's memory.

With tears in his eyes, Jay stood up in front of the empty chairs and began to speak about the wonderful times he shared with Celina. He talked about their childhood adventures, how brave she was, and the special bond they shared as siblings.

Maddison held Jay's hand tightly as he spoke, offering him the strength and support he needed during this difficult moment. As Jay finished his speech, he felt a sense of closure and peace knowing that he had paid tribute to his sister in the best way he could.

After the funeral, Jay and Maddison stood by Celina's graveside, sharing memories and reminiscing about the happy times they had all spent together. Although the funeral was not attended by many others, Jay knew that Celina's spirit would live on in the hearts of those who loved her.

As they left the cemetery, Jay felt a sense of gratitude for having Maddison by his side throughout the entire process. He knew that with her love and support, he would be able to find a way to move forward and keep his sister's memory alive in his heart forever.

4 months later-

Maddison stared at her reflection in the mirror, transfixed by the red glow in her eyes. She couldn't believe it - she was now a vampire, blood empire. Just four months ago, she was just a regular blood witch, using her powers to cast spells and brew potions. But now, everything had changed.

Maddison was scared and confused about her newfound abilities. But Jay was there to guide her, teaching her about the ways of the vampire world.

Living together in a secluded house on the outskirts of town, Maddison and Jay immersed themselves in their new lives. Jay showed Maddison how to feed on blood without harming humans, how to move swiftly and silently through the night, and how to use her heightened senses to her advantage.

As the weeks passed, Maddison grew more confident in her abilities. She and Jay would spend nights hunting together, their bond growing stronger with each passing day. They shared stories of their past lives, finding solace in each other's company.

Despite the darkness of their new existence, Maddison felt a sense of liberation. She was no longer bound by the restrictions of her previous life as a only blood witch. As the blood empire, she felt powerful, untethered, and free.

One night, as they sat under the stars, Jay turned to Maddison with a smile. "You've come a long way." he said, his eyes twinkling with pride. "I can't even explain how much i love you right now.

Maddison's heart swelled with gratitude. She knew that she had chosen the right choice. And as they sat together, watching the moon rise in the sky, they both fell in each others arms kissing each other. Maddison knew that she had found a companion for eternity.

Epilogue

2018 February 10

4 years later-

Jay and Maddison had been together for four years, and their love had only grown stronger with each passing day. They had always dreamed of having a home together, a place they could call their own. That dream finally became a reality when they purchased a beautiful and spacious house in Santiago, a city they both loved.

As they settled into their new home, Maddison began to feel unwell. At first, she brushed it off as just a bug or a passing illness. But as the days went on, she knew there was something more going on. She couldn't shake the feeling that something was not quite right, she started thinking, what if she was pregnant.

"Jay! I'm going to the store, you need something?" She asks him. He nodded no and she quickly goes to the store. She quickly grabs a pregnancy test and pays. She had no reason to suspect she was pregnant, but something inside her told her to take the test.

1 hour later-

As she waited for the results, her heart raced with anticipation. When she finally looked at the test, her heart skipped a beat. She was pregnant. She couldn't believe it. Her hands were shaking? she was going to be a mother, and Jay was going to be a father.

She couldn't wait to share the news with him, but she wanted to do it in a special way.

That evening, as they sat down for dinner, Maddison couldn't keep the news to herself any longer. She took a deep breath and looked into Jay's eyes. "I have something to tell you," she said, her voice trembling with excitement. "I'm pregnant.

"Jay's eyes widened with surprise, and then a smile broke out on his face. "Really?" he exclaimed, his voice filled with joy. "Thats just.. unbelievable. So this means i'm going to be a father."

"And i'm sure we will be amazing parents."

"They both hugged each other tightly, feeling a rush of emotions wash over them. They were going to be parents, and their lives were about to change in the best possible way.

As the weeks went by, Maddison's pregnancy progressed smoothly. Jay was by her side every step of the way, supporting her and taking care of her as she prepared for the arrival of their little one, she was pregnant for one month right now.

8 months later-

Maddison's pregnancy had been a smooth journey thus far, filled with excitement and anticipation for the arrival of their first child. As the due date approached, Maddison and Jay were eagerly preparing for the big day. They had set up the nursery, attended prenatal classes, and made sure everything was in order for their little one's arrival.

One evening, as Maddison was resting on the couch watching TV, she suddenly felt a sharp pain in her abdomen. She winced in discomfort and realized that her water had broken. "Jay!" Panic set in as she realized that their baby could be coming sooner than expected. Jay sprang into action, grabbing their hospital bag and helping Maddison to her feet. They rushed out the door and into the car, racing towards the hospital with adrenaline coursing through their veins.

As they arrived at the hospital, Maddison was taken to the labor and delivery ward while Jay filled out the necessary paperwork. The nurses quickly assessed Maddison and confirmed that she was indeed in labor. Jay held Maddison's hand tightly, offering words of encouragement as she braced herself for the intense contractions that were sure to come.

Hours passed and Maddison's contractions grew stronger and closer together. She squeezed Jay's hand tightly, gritting her teeth through each wave of pain. The medical team was monitoring her progress closely, ensuring that both she and the baby were safe and healthy throughout the labor process.

Finally, after what felt like an eternity, Maddison was ready to start pushing. With Jay by her side, cheering her on every step of the way, Maddison gave it her all. The room was filled with the sounds of her grunts and the nurses' encouraging words as they coached her through each push.

And then, after one final, powerful push, their baby girl entered the world. The room seemed to hold its breath as the cry of their newborn filled the air. Tears of joy streamed down Jay's face as the nurse placed their baby girl on Maddison's chest for the first time. "She looks just like you Jay." Maddison says Jay as she holds the baby, the baby had ice blue eyes and a little amount of black hair. "She reminds me of Celina, how do we call her?" Jay asks looking at the baby happy. "Her name will be Celine."